# A SHOT OF SIN

## EDEN SUMMERS

*To passion and love.*
*To naughtiness and risk.*

# CHAPTER ONE

"*R*aspberry and vodka, thanks. And in a tall glass this time."

Shay Porter acknowledged the order with a nod and prepared the guy's drink with the last shot of vodka in the bottle. The man was a loner. Three nights a week, every week, he came to Shot of Sin. He ordered the same girlie beverage, chatted up same high-class women and then went home sulking, as if he was the only one here who hadn't anticipated the rejection.

Dumb fucker.

"Do you want a straw with that?" she called over the heavy club music, her smile insincere.

His hazel eyes narrowed. "The drink is for me," he snarled and handed her the correct change.

She turned her back with a shrug and placed the money in the register. "Still a legitimate question, asshole," she muttered, retrieving the empty liquor bottle from the overhead dispenser.

"Taunting the customers again, Shay?"

Her spine tingled at the gravel-rich tone. Leo Petrova, aka

1

Mr. Boss Man, was one sexy hunk of masculinity. Skin tanned from an unending kiss of the Beaumont, Texas sun, hair long enough to be pulled into a short ponytail with wisps falling around his face to highlight intense blue-green eyes.

*Change of panties needed at the main bar, please.*

"He can't expect to score when he orders girlie drinks like that." She dumped the empty bottle in the bin beside his sexy muscled legs covered in coal Chino's. When she lifted her gaze over his white buttoned shirt and met his focus, she subtly licked her lips, inwardly rejoicing at his narrowed gaze. She had to do these little things—smile seductively, plump her breasts, accidentally trip over invisible objects and find herself plastered against his body. How else could she weaken his defenses? "The single women think he's gay. I can't stand to watch the carnage anymore."

She turned on her heel and headed for the storeroom, hoping Leo would follow. As she flicked on the light in the darkened room behind the bar, she smiled, sensing his dominant presence at her back.

"Then quit." He slid the door closed behind them, lessening the harsh thrum of music.

Quit? No.

Under the thick layers of his hard-ass bravado, he was joking. She knew that. And he knew she would never leave. She loved working at Shot of Sin and the adjoining restaurant, Taste of Sin. This place was her second home. The bar staff she managed might not always appreciate her temperamental attitude, but her three bosses valued her contributions... Well, most of the time.

More importantly, they listened to her suggestions on improving the business. After five years of hopping from one employer to the next, she'd finally found a place worth sticking to. The eye candy her boss provided was an added bonus.

2

She glanced over her shoulder with a raised brow. Her body hummed with his proximity. What she wouldn't give for him to push her against the side of the shelves and make her whimper in pleasure.

He leaned against the wall, arms crossed over his chest. "We've spoken about your sassy mouth before. Either stop it, or take a walk."

She cleared her throat to cover a chuckle. "Is that how you plan to work around the no-sleeping-with-staff policy?" She turned to the shelves in search of another vodka bottle. "Fire me so you can have your way with me? 'Cause I'm okay with that, as long as I'm a kept woman."

His growl reverberated off the walls, making her nipples burn.

"Don't push me tonight, Shayna."

No nickname? Two points for getting under his skin.

"Or what?" She retrieved a bottle from the high shelf and faced him. "You know you won't fire me. I'm the hardest worker you've got." And hopefully the only one he was attracted to.

She stepped forward, bringing them toe-to-toe. His gaze held her captive, staring her down. She knew he wouldn't break the connection. One, because Mr. Dominant would never heel to a woman. And two, because she had the impression his aversion to kissing her weakened if he glanced lower to her lips. Or better still, to the cleavage he liked to eye-fuck whenever he thought she wasn't watching. "I'm sure you could shut this sassy mouth without the threat of sacking me."

His nostrils flared. There was attraction in those ocean eyes, no doubt about it. Only she knew he wouldn't act upon it. Not yet, anyway. He'd made it clear their first heated interlude had been a mistake. It wouldn't stop her from taunting him with something she was more than willing to give, though. One day she'd break through his no-relationships barrier, she just had to be patient.

He leaned in, positioning his mouth deliciously close to her ear, making her skin prickle with awareness. "I could shut you up, little girl, but I'd be scared of choking you with this big dick of mine."

Shay pressed her lips together, fighting the burst of laughter threatening to break free. "I've got an exceptional gag reflex." She let the vodka bottle fall between them, the heavy weight brushing his crotch.

Voices echoed from the bar and Leo stiffened, moving out of reach moments before the second boss in the trio of broodish men slid the door open. T.J. frowned as he cautiously entered the room. His brown-eyed gaze narrowed on Leo before turning Shay's way.

"This doesn't look inappropriate at all," he drawled. "What are you two doing back here?"

Shay held up the liquor bottle in her hand. "I came to get a refill. I'm not entirely sure why he followed."

Leo rolled his eyes. "What do you want?"

T.J. shook his head with a knowing grin and turned his attention to Leo. "Tracy broke her arm. She's going to be out of action for a while."

"Tracy?" Shay frowned.

"She works downstairs."

Ahh. The illusive VIP lounge she'd never been allowed to step foot in. Apparently, being the most valued employee upstairs didn't hold enough merit to see where all the beautiful people went each Saturday night.

"We don't have anyone to replace her shift next week when Travis is away," T.J. continued. "Bryan and I thought Shay could take her place."

Shay's eyes widened, not only at the new opportunity, but more shockingly that Bryan, aka Brute, would suggest she was capable of such a highly-coveted role. He'd earned his nickname because of the harsh way he dealt with life. He was merciless, clinical, and rarely showed emotion. Most of the time, he was an accomplished grump who liked to hide any enthusiasm under snarky insults. This suggestion proved her theory that underneath all the angst, he truly was a soft, cuddly bear.

Like hell she was going to point out the uncharacteristic comment though. Downstairs intrigued her. She'd already spent months in the adjoining Taste of Sin restaurant earning their respect before they'd let her work in the dance club part of the business. Now she wanted to hit the big time. The door leading to the private part of the club was always protected each Saturday by a security guard. Not even long-term Shot of Sin staff could enter, and she'd never met anyone who worked behind the sacred walls.

"No." Leo's tone brooked no argument.

"Excuse me?" She straightened her shoulders and raised a brow. She wasn't a daddy's girl or a wealthy socialite who expected her every whim to be adhered to, but when it came to devaluing her, in any way, her hackles immediately rose.

"I said no." He turned his focus to T.J. "I don't want her down there."

"What's your problem?" she snapped. Yes, he was her stubborn, slightly nauseatingly gorgeous boss, but they were meant to be friends. Even more if he'd finally lower his guard and allow it. And now he was treating her as if she couldn't handle a simple night's work at a different bar.

"She isn't trained to work in that environment." He no longer acknowledging her presence. "We'll find someone else."

T.J.'s brow furrowed. "Shay, can you give us a sec?"

She held tight to the liquor bottle in her fist. "Fine." Clenching her teeth together, she fixed her arrogant fantasy with a glare and then pushed past him to the open doorway. "Convince him, T.J. Otherwise, you might find yourself looking to replace more than one staff member."

~

*L*eo watched Shay's ass storm from the storeroom and then winced when she slammed the sliding door. The woman drove him crazy. She was wild and sassy with a delectable body capable of making his cock twitch on a hair-trigger. She was also predictable. Now that she was sporting a mammoth case of fury, he knew she'd go back to work and bat her lashes at every pretentious asshole in the building just to piss him off.

In other words, she was trouble. And as drawn to her as he was, he didn't need another complication in his life. The restaurant and bar kept him, T.J. and Brute busy, and with the private club downstairs increasing its clientele, none of them needed a distraction. Especially one with pretty light-brown eyes and dark wavy hair.

"Give me one good reason why she can't work down there," T.J. muttered, the shadowed smudges under his eyes more prominent than earlier in the evening.

"Like I said, she hasn't been trained."

"And like I said, give me one good reason."

Fuck. Leo let out a heavy breath and wiped a hand down his face. "I just don't want her down there, okay?"

T.J. and Brute weren't aware he'd once succumbed to her sassy charm. He'd practically dry-humped her in this very room—his tongue down her throat, his fingers in her panties, sliding through her slick juices. He'd strode away soon after she'd climaxed around his digits, his jaw tight with regret. Unbeknown to Shay, she'd proven she wasn't what he needed, no matter how much she thought she was. His sexual appetite was raw, demanding, and not suitable for someone with a narrow scope on pleasure.

In the few moments they'd shared, he'd seen her innocence. She wasn't a virgin by any means, but neither was she a female equipped to handle his desires. She'd gasped at his ferocity, stared at him like he was an entirely different man, and he'd learned long ago to back away when his needs didn't match those of the woman he was interested in. Things would only become complicated later. Been there, done that.

He had the emotional scars to prove it.

So, he'd run, and hoped T.J. and Brute didn't hear about his fuck up. For weeks, he'd distanced himself from the hope of commitment in her eyes. He'd hated fracturing the defenses of such a strong-willed woman, only he hadn't had a choice. With her penchant for tantrums, he'd had to snap out of the attraction in an instant. Or at least pretend to.

"Unfortunately, with the limited staff employed downstairs, we don't have any other options. Travis has already scheduled annual leave and I'm not going back on my word when it's the anniversary of his dad's death." T.J. huffed in frustration. "Look, I know you have a thing for her, but you've gotta decide—are you her manager or the guy who wants to get in her pants?"

Leo scowled. "I don't want to get in her pants." Been there, done that, too.

"Then why is it a hard decision?"

Sadly, when it came to the sassy wench, things were always hard. For Leo, anyway. Problem was he didn't have a legitimate excuse to stop her from getting them out of the staffing issue.

"Fine." He stabbed his fingers through his hair, loosening his ponytail. "But I'll be the one to show her around. Brute can take my shift up here next Saturday and I'll take his downstairs."

T.J. shrugged. "I'm cool with that. You could take her down tonight if you wanted. We aren't likely to get overrun up here."

Leo's palms began to sweat. "Yeah, okay."

He closed his eyes and rubbed the back of his lids. Shay didn't have a good track record of reacting with professional calm when surprised. And the contrasting environment downstairs would definitely be a bombshell.

One of his pet peeves was judgement from others, especially friends and family. Yes, it was human nature for every fucker to have an opinion, even when the situations they were criticizing were none of their goddamn business. He was just sick to death of narrow-minded people opening their mouths and spewing hatred about shit they didn't understand. He didn't know how he'd handle that type of commentary from Shay. And she'd definitely have an opinion about the activities in the downstairs area.

"You sure this doesn't have anything to do with you wanting to slam your cock down her throat?"

"Christ, T.J." Leo scowled. "Don't you think downstairs would be the first place I'd take her if I did?"

"Just askin'." He held up his hands in surrender and backtracked to the door.

"Well, don't." Leo jerked his head toward the hall and hoped T.J. would leave him the hell alone so he could think shit through. "Look after the main floor tonight. Leave Shay to me."

# CHAPTER TWO

*S*hay raised a questioning brow at T.J. as he strode behind the bar toward her. He waited until she finished serving one of the bleach-blonde regulars before sidling up beside her.

"You okay?" he asked, always the gentleman.

She liked T.J. He was sweet, caring and always had her back, even when she didn't deserve it. His dark features and drool-worthy appearance didn't hinder her fondness for him, either. She doubted there was a woman who entered Shot of Sin who hadn't fantasized about him, or the other two owners. And if the women were anything like Shay, they'd fantasized about all three of the men at the same time, because she was creative like that. Only now, she was too pissed off to appreciate the gorgeousness of T.J.'s dark-brown eyes.

"I suppose that depends." She wiped her hands on her jean-covered hips and eyed the bar staff to make sure they didn't become overrun with drink orders. "Is Leo committed to being a jerk?"

"He's only looking out for you."

"Bullshit." She met his gaze with a glare. She'd been through this before, having worked with more than one manager who didn't believe she was as capable as her male counterparts. There was no way she would allow her time here to go down the same path. "I've never disappointed you. Not once. Yet, Leo's initial instinct is to claim I'm incapable of handling new duties. Christ, T.J., how hard could it be? I rarely see anyone go down there."

T.J. winced while his focus strayed over her shoulder. Moments later, Brute strolled up beside them and leaned against the back counter as staff members buzzed around them.

"What's going on?" His blue eyes were devoid of expression. As always. The dark-blond, clean-cut beard also helped to hide any emotions he had going on in that stubborn face of his. "Did you ask Shay about working downstairs?"

"We were just discussing it," T.J. muttered over the music. "Leo was a little apprehensive about the suggestion, but I think I won him over."

"Won him over?" Shay bit out. "He shouldn't need to be won over. I'm the most capable bartender you have."

T.J. and Brute exchanged a glance she suspected held hidden meaning.

"What?" she asked. "Aren't you happy with the way I've been running things?"

"No. It's not that." T.J.'s response was immediate. "Leo's being protective. Downstairs isn't as..."

"Straight," Brute added. "It'll definitely keep you on your toes."

Shay focused on them both in turn. T.J. no longer made eye contact. His attention hovered anywhere but her face, as if he were apprehensive, or maybe nervous. Brute met her gaze head on, but his vacant expression gave nothing away.

"I can handle it." At the very least, she deserved the

opportunity to prove herself. She only wished Leo had as much faith in her as T.J. and Brute.

"I know you can." T.J squeezed her shoulder. "Leo does too. He's just a little touchy when it comes to downstairs."

*Touchy* she could handle. What she couldn't stand was the hit to her pride from a guy she had a female boner for.

"I better go check that Taste of Sin closed properly. I'll catch you both later." T.J. gave her shoulder another gentle squeeze and then made his way around the bar.

Shay watched him disappear into the crowd of dancing bodies and cursed herself for crushing on the wrong bar owner. Leo was too stubborn. The only problem was that he was exactly what she wanted in a guy. Apart from having the ability to melt her panties with a single glance, he was confident, capable and too deliciously sexy when he growled at her.

Their one scorching play session in the bar storeroom had been enough to cement her attraction to him. Confident and capable, Leo always exuded dominance and possession. Shay was certain he'd be the same in the sack. A wicked combination to tempt a woman who had never truly been satisfied by the opposite sex...or the same sex for that matter.

"So what's the real problem here? Are you annoyed at Leo for not giving you the job opportunity, or are you pissed because he won't sleep with you?"

Shay turned her gaze back to Brute with a gaping mouth. "You really need to research social filters."

"Why? We're close enough to cut the crap and I'm not going to waste my time dancing around the topic."

Of course he wouldn't. Brute was the type to take pleasure in asking the questions nobody wanted to voice. "His aversion to sleeping with me has nothing to do with my annoyance." She used the term loosely. They all knew she tended to bypass the annoyance stage and head straight to fury. "I can work any bar. Leo's just being an ass."

"Fair enough." Brute shrugged, seeming unconvinced. "I'll leave you to it. So don't sweat the simple stuff, sweetheart. If he hasn't changed his mind by closing time, me and Mr. Attitude will have a chat."

Even though he wasn't the guy her libido craved, the term of endearment made her heart flutter. He may have been nicknamed for his brutality, but it didn't stop her from searching for the soft and gooey center he pretended not to have. The guy had a heart. Somewhere. He just didn't like to show it.

Brute strode away at the same time she noticed Leo standing in the doorway leading to the storeroom. His gaze was fixed on her, his jaw tight, chin raised. In an instant, the heart fluttering began to pound, from fury or attraction, she wasn't sure.

She turned her back, unable to look at him without losing the last of her withering professionalism. Fucking asshole. His appeal defied logic. Not only was he worthy of naming rights to her vibrator, she was pretty sure toy manufacturers would kill to mold the package outlined in the crotch of his butt-hugging Chino's. The annoying part was that he wasn't just a panty-wetting machine due to his looks. He actually had a surprisingly enjoyable personality—for a male. Well, he used to. He used to be playful and flirty and charming...until the night he slid his hand into her pants and then backed away like he'd armed a bomb.

"Now I'm just another easy bar wench."

"Excuse me?" He came up behind her, his shadow falling over her shoulder.

She turned and pinned him with a death stare. "I said, get out of my face."

He raised a brow, the side of his heart-stopping lips tilting. "You're quick to bite my head off tonight."

She scoffed and nudged passed him. "Yeah, and funnily enough, you're the one acting like you've got PMS." She strode around the bar and into the dancing crowd illuminated in purple light. This time, she hoped he didn't follow. She needed space from all his self-assured gorgeousness, and she was owed a twenty-minute break.

Palming the phone in her pocket to make sure it didn't fall out, she bumped through the mass of gyrating bodies and headed toward the opposite side of the building. As she approached the guarded entrance to the fancy-schmancy private club, she scowled at the guard manning the door. It wasn't his fault she was crabby, but the fucks she gave about who took the brunt of her anger were nowhere to be found.

"*Shay*," Leo yelled over the heavy pulse of music. "Hold up."

She paused, crossing her arms over her chest like a petulant child.

"You really want to go down there?" he asked over her shoulder.

She turned on him. "It's not about wanting to go down there." She raised her voice, hoping it didn't waiver. "It's about you not giving a shit about how hard I work. I'm the one who stays late to help clean up." She tapped her chest with a pointed finger. "I'm the one who works overtime in the restaurant if someone calls in sick." *Tap*. "I'm the one all the regulars come to because they know I remember their drink order." She poked him in the sternum. "Your attitude is a kick in the face to all the effort I put in."

Leo glanced around with disinterest. "You finished?"

"Do I look like I'm finished?" she grated and then thought better of continuing the hissy fit when clearly he didn't care. "Forget it."

Turning, she pushed passed a couple making out and stormed for the nearest exit. As she strode by the guard at the private entrance, a hand grabbed her upper arm, pulling her back.

"Hey, Jeff, you mind letting us in?" Leo asked.

The colossal guard's brows knitted as his gaze lowered to the grip tightening on her arm. "Sure thing, boss."

He pushed open the bulky door and stepped to the side, eyeing them with concern as Leo hauled her into the darkness. When the door closed, Shay's heart rocketed into her throat.

In here, it was quieter, almost deafeningly so, and the faint thump, thump, thump of bass barely breached the walls. The light from the club had been extinguished too, making her eyes work to adjust to an even darker environment.

A quick glimpse to her left showed a narrow staircase with crimson wallpaper lining the walls and plush carpet under her feet. The area was more compact than she imagined, more intimate, especially when she stood toe-to-toe with a man who stole her breath.

"You know your grip is bordering on harassment."

His hand fell away as she gazed up into his shadowed features.

"Sorry," he murmured. "I didn't expect you to throw a tantrum."

Tantrum? "If I wasn't furious right now, I'd be belting you with a plethora of insults."

She shouldered him out of the way, no longer giving a shit about what treasures lurked below. He could take his private club and shove it where rich people didn't shine. She was a fucking brilliant bartender, and if Leo didn't appreciate her skills, she might have to leave and find a bar owner who did.

Stupid lust-filled crush be damned.

She gripped the door handle and plunged the leaver, but

as soon as she pulled, Leo wrapped a strong arm around her waist. Time stopped, along with her breathing, while the heat of his chest invaded her lungs. She could smell his sweet, exotic aftershave. Could feel his warm exhalations tickling her neck as she fought to keep her posture straight and defiant.

"Being a great employee has nothing to do with my reasons for not wanting you in here," he hissed under his breath.

She raised her chin, hating the way her core contracted and her nipples beaded beneath her bra. "Then why?"

He dropped his arm from her waist and the heat from his body disappeared. She turned in the silence, wishing she could make out his face clearly as he stepped back.

"Why, Leo?"

The sparing dim lights stretching along the ceiling didn't reach the far corner where he stood. She couldn't see his eyes, only the faint jut of his chin and his straightened shoulders. She could sense a bravado settling over him, yet she had no clue why.

"This game we play..." he started, leaning back to rest against the wall. "I enjoy it. The banter, the tension. Even the way your flirting grabs hold of my dick and won't let go." He paused, as if sensing she needed a moment to let his words sink in. "I don't want to ruin that."

Her heart lurched. "Okay..."

She'd never played games. Every time she'd flirted, she'd done it with intent, with the sole focus of not only getting in his bed, but in his heart. She sure as shit wasn't going to correct him though. Not when he was being such an ass. "Where is this speech going? You've already made it crystal you don't want to be with me, so why all the dramatics?"

Silence. Then there was a long, drawn-out sigh that dried her throat.

"Follow me."

He started down the stairs, and she cursed herself for following behind so quickly. No matter how willing she'd been to walk out the door, curiosity still won. She needed to know what was at the end of the staircase.

As they descended, crisp, cool air danced around her heels, filtered in through air vents near the floor. The atmosphere was different to the bubbly purple and silver of the main area of Shot of Sin. In here, she struggled to fight unease. She could see picture frames lining the walls, and when they reached the first, she stopped and did a double-take. She expected a landscape, or maybe autographed images from people who'd made their way into this exclusive part of the club. But it was neither.

The first frame held a black and white photograph of a naked couple, intimately entwined. It was erotic, graphic, and when Leo glanced over his shoulder, she felt like she'd been caught with a hand in her own private cookie jar.

The beauty of the image made her feel inadequate. Here she was in a tight black Shot-of-Sin tank and jeans, while they bared their bodies and souls for art. It was spectacular and oddly confounding. Why would Leo, T.J., or even Brute for that matter, pick out something so graphic to decorate their private club?

She shook away the confusion and followed after the sculpted shoulders continuing down the stairs. More images passed by, all with couples in erotic poses—men with women, women with women, and more delicious than she would've imagined, muscled men with sexy muscled men. Each shot was beautiful in its own striking way, but now Shay was beyond bewildered and heading for freak-out central.

The darkness, the silence, the sex lining the walls, it set her fertile mind to work on some pretty heavy ideas. By the time she reached the last step, she was staring at Leo's back in contemplation, her palms sweating and not from exertion. Finally, his warnings had sunk in, and she thought better of pushing him to the point of dragging her down here. For the first time since becoming an independent adult, she felt anxious.

"That's the locker room."

Leo's voice startled her, and she glanced from his back to see him pointing to a closed door highlighted with one small light above the frame.

"Patrons are encouraged to leave valuables at home, but everything else gets locked up in there."

"Everything else?" She tagged along behind him.

He ignored her, not faltering in his dominant stride as he pointed to another closed door. "And that is the change room."

"Change room?" she asked louder. "What is all this for?"

He continued to the end of the hall, to a padded door bathed in glowing light. A keypad was positioned on the wall at chest height, the numbers aglow in bright blue. She glanced from the keypad to the back of Leo's head with growing apprehension. What required all this secrecy and security?

"Are you going to answer me?" Her voice waivered.

He always had a quick word to say. In fact, he usually had the final word in every conversation, yet now he was silent. *Toot toot.* All aboard the freak-out train.

"Leo?"

He turned to her and waved a lazy arm toward the door. "This is what you wanted."

She couldn't tear her gaze from him. She was looking for a clue, a tiny hint to make her laugh off the impending heart attack. Only, in the brighter light, she could see the worry around his eyes, the troubling furrow to his brow.

"Ladies first."

He indicated for her to step in front and she reluctantly complied. Once she was a foot away from the door, he moved behind her, leaned close, and hovered his fingers over the keypad.

"On the other side of the door isn't just a VIP lounge. It's an exclusive club, something someone like you wouldn't be familiar with."

*Someone like me?*

Now he was trying to make her feel inferior for not being wealthy or famous? She turned her head, glaring at the side of his face. "Insult me one more time..."

"And what?" His mouth quirked and he met her stare with a raised brow.

She got in his face, close enough she was caught between wanting to slam her fist into his perfect nose or smash her mouth against his. "And I'll..." She bit back her anxiety-riddled reply. "Don't worry, Leo," she snarled his name. "I won't embarrass you in front of whatever pretentious, high-powered people you have in there."

He chuckled, soft and low. "It's not them I'm worried about."

Before she could question his comment, his fingers were on the keypad, entering a four-digit number. The door buzzed, and he flung it wide. A fresh burst of cool air filtered forward, and her eyes widened, not only at the porn playing on the huge television in front of her, but at the unmistakable sounds of sex that weren't coming through in Dolby digital quality. Oh no, the noises she heard were real-life, unscripted feminine moans and brutal grunts coming from another room.

*Holy shit.*

"Welcome to Vault of Sin, Shay," he drawled.

Her mouth worked, unable to form words as her gaze went in search of where the lust-filled sounds were coming from. "Is this a brothel?" she blurted, her focus now glued to the woman being hammered on screen by two men.

"No."

"A sex club?" Her voice was suddenly high-pitched.

"Surprise." He nudged her into the room and closed the door behind them.

Holy adolescent hormones.

Her mouth gaped. How had she not known this was going on right underneath her feet? And for how long? Shay glanced around in a daze, scoping out the small room with an archway at the far wall. Apart from the screen full of orgasmic undulation, there was a leather sofa, a dimly lit lamp, and a basket in the corner with items she wasn't sure she wanted to know about.

"This is the chill-out room." Leo strode forward, heading for the archway. "A place for newbies to settle in before joining the fun."

Fun?

She released an awkward chuckle.

Leo's relaxed stride added to her horror. She tried not to contemplate how many hours it would take to become nonchalant about this type of setting. How many women he'd seen. How many orgasms he'd heard. She shook her head, ignoring the bite of jealousy nipping at her ribs, the cloying adrenaline rushing through her veins, and the slight buzz of arousal.

"You coming?" He stood at the archway with a raised brow.

"Obviously not right at this very moment." She straightened her shoulders and took pleasure in the way Leo's gaze lowered to her breasts. He was smart enough to figure out she was fighting her discomfort through sarcasm, and she didn't have the sense to care. It was the only reliable strategy she had to calm down and stop her from rushing back up those stairs. "It takes more than porn to get this motor running."

"If memory serves, it can take a lot less."

*Argh*.

How did he do that? Take all the rushing emotions flowing through her body and replace them instantly with the need to choke him.

Ignoring his deep chuckle, she ground her teeth and strengthened her resolve as she came up behind him. Together, they stepped into a larger room and her knees threatened to give out. She'd tried to prepare herself, yet her imagination hadn't been equipped to create the cavern of carnality before her.

There were beds. A hammock. Leather sofas. A sex swing. And half were occupied with writhing naked bodies. Numerous television screens played different porn scenes while the bar stood alone in the back corner, the only surface in the room currently safe from copulation.

The whimpers, groans, grunts and screams hit her like physical blows, making her step back, dizzy with adrenaline. She didn't know where to look—at the huge cock plowing into the woman to her right, the spread thighs of the female giving head to a muscle-ripped black guy, or the safe and easy bartender who polished a glass, unfazed by the room filled with the smell of sex and sweat.

"Ready to put your tail between your legs and run back upstairs?" Leo taunted.

She raised her chin. "Bite me."

Asshole.

He gave a predatory chuckle and leaned into her, his lips brushing her ear. "You're in my territory now, Shay. Don't tempt me with dares I'd be more than willing to fulfill."

Her knees weakened, her breathing became labored as he turned and strutted like a fucking peacock toward the bar.

She didn't like this. Not one little bit. Upstairs, she held the upper hand. The bars were her domain. She was king of that freaking castle.

Down here was the opposite. This was Leo's territory. The way he baited her only proved how comfortable he felt in this environment. And unfortunately for her, she was entirely out of her depth.

"Leo," she scolded, trying not to distract the patrons from their...patronage.

He ignored her, giving her no choice but to follow in his footsteps like a lost puppy. She came up beside him at the bar, still shaking and skittish when he placed his hand at the low of her back and indicated to the bartender unpacking the dishwasher under the counter.

"Travis, this is Shay."

The mocha-skinned man threw his dishcloth on the counter and hit her with a seductive grin. "Hey, Shay." He held out a hand. "Welcome to the fun house."

She shook his hand, letting the warmth of his palm soothe her, holding on longer than necessary for the support.

"Don't look so petrified." His smile warmed. "You'll be okay."

She wanted to clarify, to tell him whatever horrified expression crossed her features was from shock, not cowardice, but her addled brain had packed up and left the building.

"Shay's the bar manager from upstairs," Leo interrupted, his tone gruff. "She won't be here permanently, only the remainder of tonight and next Saturday to cover Tracy's shift." He pressed his hand harder at the low of her back. "There's no hanging around after closing tonight, Travis. You feel me?"

The bartender stiffened and released Shay's hand. "No

problem." Then he turned and moved back to the middle of the bar to continue his job at the dishwasher.

It wasn't until she glanced at Leo that she realized why Travis had fled. Her boss was glaring, still focused on the guy with an unwavering feral stare. "No playing between the staff." He tilted his head, turning those hard ocean eyes on her. "Understood?"

"You're worried about me sleeping with him?" she grated. "Christ, Leo, back off." She was trying her best to remain level-headed about the switch from dance-club bartender to beverage dispenser on a porn set. But there was only so much she could take. And apparently, it wasn't as much as the woman moaning around a mouthful in the corner. She had a guy down her throat, one doing her doggie, and another caressing her breasts, trying to get in on the action.

"I'm not joking, Shay." He turned into her, gripping her chin to hold her attention captive. "No one touches you."

Why don't the rules apply to you? She wanted to ask but bit her tongue instead.

"I'm going to do a scan of the rooms and make sure everything's in order. I'll give you a full tour later, once you've digested the basics. I don't want to scar you for life."

"I've had sex before, Leo. None of this is new to me."

He smirked. "I know from experience, remember? But have you had sex like this?" He quirked a brow, waiting for her response even though the arrogant bastard already knew the answer. "Yeah, I didn't think so."

She leaned toward him, lowering her voice and adding menace to her tone. "Well, maybe I'll convince T.J. to let me down here as a guest. That way I can gain the experience you seem to think is so important." The lie flew from her mouth without pause. He kept baiting her. Her only defense was to retaliate, especially when her own body betrayed her with lust.

His eyes flashed. "You will never come down here without me. You understand? Never."

Her nipples tingled with his command. Traitorous fucking nipples. "You can walk me down those stairs as often as you like, but you've made it clear you won't be making me come again. This is the perfect place for me to find someone who will." Again, the untruths rushed forward, and this time she couldn't help the accompanying smirk.

He released his grip and the anger in his eyes increased. "Never, Shay." And then he was gone, striding away with his head held high and his shoulders straight with arrogance.

# CHAPTER THREE

*L*eo continued walking through the main area and into one of the private rooms where Shay's gaze couldn't tickle the back of his neck.

Motherfucker.

This wasn't what he'd expected. She was meant to run, to glare at him in disgust, call him a perverted asshole and vow to never come down here again. Instead, she was still a sassy-mouthed viper and the lust in her eyes hadn't dulled. She was shocked as hell, that much was clear, but she hadn't fled. And now he didn't know what to do.

This was a first for him. Every woman he'd introduced to this part of himself had done a runner. Whether he brought it up in conversation to prepare them, or they made the entire journey to the club door, they all ended up fleeing from his life. Yet, Shay had stuck around, remaining true to her typical reaction to shock—hitting him with a healthy barrage of sarcasm.

Maybe he'd misjudged her. Or maybe she was too proud to admit defeat after stamping her foot and demanding to work down here. Either way, he'd come further than he had with any other woman he'd cared about. He should be relieved, shouldn't he?

"Leo?"

He blinked the half-empty room into focus and smiled at the leggy blonde sauntering toward him. Curvy, with deep-brown eyes and flawless skin, Pamela was a sight to behold. Yet, she was the anomaly in their environment. For an attractive woman, she was shy, apprehensive and didn't like showing off the assets hidden under her shiny red corset and panties. In fact, he'd never seen her participate at all. Like T.J., she only ever watched.

"Are you playing tonight?" She came up beside him, her eyes weary.

"No, sweetheart." He couldn't play. Not with the image of Shay still firmly plastered in the forefront of his mind. "But have fun without me."

She lowered her gaze, nodded and began to slink away.

"Pamela? You okay?"

She paused, glancing over her shoulder with watery eyes.

"Pamela?"

"I'm just frustrated," she murmured. "I want to join in."

He bridged the distance between them in two steps and cupped her upper arms with an encouraging smile. "Then go for it."

"It's not that easy. I haven't been with a man since my husband died."

Husband? Leo jerked back. The beauty couldn't be older than twenty-eight. How the hell was she a widow?

"Don't look at me like that." She gave a half-hearted chuckle. "It happened almost two years ago, but I haven't been able to convince myself to..." she shrugged, "...get back on the horse." Her eyes twinkled and a soft grin tilted her lips. "Could you help me?"

Shit. Talk about insensitive. He had no idea what to say. Shay had rattled him. "What do you need?"

"Guidance." She looked at him with hope. "I know you don't want to play, but could you get me started with someone? Maybe stand beside me and give directions. My husband was very..." she paused, biting her lip, "...instructive. I loved how he took control."

Leo scrubbed a hand over his jaw, trying to wipe Shay from his mind. Tonight was getting more complicated by the minute. "Of course." He scoped the small room, looking for an unoccupied guy. Two hetro couples were in the darkened far corner, the male positioned over his partner, giving her a massage. His hands were on her back while he ground his pelvis against her naked ass. The other couple sat on a leather sofa, murmuring words between slow kisses.

"Give me a sec." He strode from the room, unable to stop his focus from wandering to Shay. She was talking to Travis, a grin plastered across her beautiful face. When her gaze found his, he glanced away, finding what he needed on the chaise to the left of the doorway.

"Jack," he barked.

The guy continued to stroke his cock as he dragged his attention from the two men pleasuring a chesty blonde in the sex swing. "Yeah?"

"I need a little help in here."

"Sure thing." Jack stood, unabashed by his nudity or the stiff dick in his hand.

Leo jerked a thumb in Pamela's direction and waited for the man to pass before he chanced another glance at Shay. Shit. Their gazes collided and her brow furrowed in a silent question. Great. Exactly what he needed—an inquisitive, sassy wench. He ignored her and turned on his heel, making sure the frustration was hidden from his expression when he reached Pamela's side.

"What's up?" Jack asked.

Leo cleared his throat to stop a smart retort and gestured to Pamela. "I want you to help me with this beautiful lady."

Pamela's cheeks turned a darker shade of pink.

"It'd be my pleasure. What do you need me to do?"

Leo waved a lazy hand at the bed to their right. "Kneel on the mattress and go with the flow."

Jack did as instructed, surveying his upcoming conquest with hungry eyes.

"Do you have any rules?" Leo swung to Pamela.

Although members did have paddles, nipple clamps, restraints and floggers at their disposal, this wasn't a BDSM club. Safe words weren't a necessity. However, Leo respected everyone's limits and wanted Pamela's first step back into the world of pleasure to be enjoyable.

She tore her focus from the bed and met Leo's gaze. "No kissing on the mouth. I'm not ready for that."

"No problem," Jack replied. "We'll do whatever you're comfortable with, and don't be scared to stop at any time."

Leo eyed the man, giving him a subtle nod in thanks. Jack had no way of knowing Pamela's history. Yet, his response was exactly what the club was all about. It wasn't all hard fucking and fulfillment. It was about growth through experience, finding likeminded people and learning about yourself as well as others. More importantly, it was about respect.

Most people were quick to judge the less-inhibited lifestyle, not taking the time to understand the safety that accompanied a controlled environment. Women didn't need to be vulnerable and bring a stranger home to experience a one-night stand. Men didn't have to offend their hook ups when they left in the morning without leaving their number. It was also a place where people like Pamela could feel comfortable taking the first step.

"Lay on the bed, sweetheart," Leo murmured.

She complied, climbing onto the mattress to rest her head on the pillows.

"I know you asked for direction, but first I want Jack to make you feel good." Leo focused on the other man. "Go down on her. Use your hands and your mouth to bring her to the brink. Just don't let her come."

Pamela whimpered, biting her beautifully straight teeth into her lower lip as she clenched her thighs together.

Jack grinned and shuffled to her side, gently spreading her legs with his large hands. He hooked his fingers under the waistband of her red satin underwear and slowly pulled them down, exposing the clean-shaven pussy beneath. "You're gorgeous." His gaze was riveted as he placed the material beside him on the mattress.

She was. Blushing with a lustful glow, her breasts heaving against the tightly strung corset, Pamela was a sight, one he hoped her deceased husband had savored.

Jack lay between her spread knees, his mouth hovering close to her core. "Relax," he purred, keeping his focus on Pamela as he swiped his tongue out to brush her clit.

She gasped at the first lick, arching her back off the bed.

Fuck.

Tonight was testing Leo on too many levels. He ached to be the one positioned between heavenly thighs, tasting the heady flavor of arousal. He closed his eyes, picturing the image on the bed with two different people. Shay would be against the pillows, her legs parted for his touch, her cream resting on the tip of his tongue. He'd lap at her, delving his fingers into her smooth heat until she started to whimper. Then he'd back off, kissing her thighs, nipping her skin until she begged him to continue, tangling her fingers in his hair, pulling at the strands.

His dick was hard as stone at the thought. Tap, tap, tapping against his zipper, pleading for release. He wanted her. Naked. Now. If he got through the night without a waver in his step from his growing case of blue balls, he'd be fucking surprised.

Pamela's moan had his eyes opening, and he grinned to find her writhing under Jack's touch. She clutched the bed sheets, her pelvis raised for more, her sounds increasing with every flick of her lover's tongue.

"Enough," Leo ordered, his tone harsher than anticipated.

Jack growled, Pamela whimpered, and they both looked at him with annoyance.

"On your hands and knees, sweetheart." Leo softened the command. "I want you to take his dick in your mouth."

Pamela swallowed as she pushed to a seated position and Jack moved to his knees. Her sights were set on the thick erection jutting toward her, a large fist slowly pumping the length.

"Can you..." she turned to Leo and grimaced, "...can you instruct me?"

He inclined his head, his throat too dry to speak. He could still feel the shiver of Shay's gaze on his skin, could sense her nearby, could almost smell her. His blood rushed with lust and adrenaline, his forehead beaded with sweat. Never had he fought so hard with his self-control. He wanted to stride to the bar, to kiss the sass right out of her and sink his cock into her heat until she screamed.

"T-take." Fuck. He cleared his throat. "Take the head of his shaft in your mouth."

His own dick threatened to explode. He could imagine Shay's lips around his length, her tongue brushing the underside, her delicate hands cupping his balls. Without thought, he stepped forward and palmed the back of Pamela's head, guiding her, testing her gag reflex as she took Jack to the back of her throat.

With his other hand, he adjusted his erection, trying to

make the fucker comfortable when it was hard enough to drill through stone. His breathing grew heavy and his eyes rolled to the back of his head as he listened to the suction of her mouth.

Jack began to groan with each gently guided stroke, and the pressure increased to breaking point in Leo's sac. He released his grip, fumbling back as he opened his eyes.

"Are you all right if Jack takes it from here?" he asked. Guilt built in his chest, but unless he got out of this room, away from sex and the temptation of Shay, he was going to make a fool of himself.

Pamela released the cock in her mouth with a pop. "Yes." The word was breathy, her smile genuine.

Thank fuck. He stroked her loose hair behind her ear, letting the sense of achievement dilute some of his lust. "If you need anything, find me."

She nodded as Jack's hand raked through her hair, his palm guiding her mouth back to his cock.

Leo spun around, eager to flee from the potent scent of sex, and found Shay leaning against the doorframe. His cock jerked. His heart stopped. She stood with her chin raised, her jaw tense, her brows pulled together, with her arms crossed over her chest.

*You are fucking kidding me.*

She had pissed off written all over her face, and although he was thankful her blatant jealousy made his dick wilt, he didn't need her to cause a scene. Downstairs was low drama. Anyone who caused trouble was booted without a second thought and never allowed re-entry. He didn't want that to happen to Shay, because there was no way T.J. or Brute would allow him to make an exception for her behavior. No matter how much they all liked her. The trust of their patrons was paramount.

As he approached, she parted her lips and he shook his head in warning. "Think before you speak, Shay."

She narrowed her eyes and pushed from the doorframe, straightening. "I only wanted to ask a question," she cooed, her tone sweet yet full of menace. "Is that all right?"

"Sure," he muttered.

The need to slam her against the wall, cup her cheeks and kiss the look of defiance off her face was cloying. He wanted to fist her hair, to pull her head back and make sure she knew who was in control down here.

"I was just wondering what job description you file on your tax return," she spoke softly. "Before tonight, I would've considered you a businessman, but after watching your little show, you could also be defined as a pim—"

He grabbed her wrist and yanked her to his side, his eyes burning with anger. "Finish that sentence and we're done." His nostrils flared, his chest pounded, and through it all, he wished she would see past her misconceptions and understand him for who he was.

This was the reason why he hadn't wanted her down here. This was why he'd fought hard to have another staff member take over the vacant shift. He didn't care what any of the other upstairs bartenders thought of him. But with Shay, it was different.

"Don't you dare judge me," he ground out.

Her eyes glinted as he continued to hold her wrist. He could feel her pain, understand her sense of betrayal, yet there was no future for her at Shot of Sin if she didn't get over it.

"This is who I am," he grated. "I don't need your judgment. If you don't like it, you know where the fucking door is."

Her forehead creased into a mass of wrinkles and her bottom lip quavered. He lessened his grip as she fought for

31

control, raised her chin and took a deep breath. She yanked her arm free, gave him one last tortured look and then stormed away, heading for the bar.

Goddamn it.

"And that's why I'm single," he muttered, shaking his head as he made his way to the next private room.

# CHAPTER FOUR

*A*n hour later, Shay was still sulking. She knew it. Travis knew it. And wherever Leo was, he knew it too. She wasn't to blame though. Drooling over a man for months and then finding him doing whatever the hell he was doing was reason for any heart-fractured woman to lose a little composure. Well...a lot of composure. She still winced every time she ran the conversation over in her mind. The look on Leo's face when she almost called him a pimp would haunt her for a damn long time.

She hadn't meant to be such a bitch. Her emotions were out of control. He'd walked into view, demanded a naked and fully aroused man follow him into one of the rooms, and her curiosity had been piqued. Along with her jealousy.

With growing dread and an unhealthy amount of unencouraged arousal, she'd watched him from the doorway. Her heart had pounded like unforgiving thunder as he'd focused on another woman's pussy. Her eyes had burned from the erection straining against his zipper. But it was the way he gently cradled the woman's head, guiding her with adoration as she deep throated another guy that made her throat painfully tight.

Shay's confidence had dwindled with every one of Leo's heavy inhalations until she'd been a mass of mental insults. Why was this woman able to gain his attention when Shay had only been able to keep it for mere moments? Maybe her breasts weren't big enough. Maybe she was too short or made herself appear too eager. Damn him. Whatever it was, she had to get over herself. No man had the right to make her feel worthless.

Fuck that.

After next weekend, she would gladly take her position behind the upstairs main bar, tail between her legs, and never shamelessly flirt with him again. Curiosity had not only killed the cat, it had slaughtered the optimistic anticipation in her pussy, too.

"How you doing?" Travis turned his back to the room and resting against the counter.

She shrugged. Anger had made it easier to get over the shock of what was happening in the room. The blood rushing through her ears dimmed the animalistic sounds of sex, and the constant slow stream of drink requests kept her busy. Still, all she could think about was Leo and what was going through his mind.

"I'm okay." She jerked her chin to the left. "The guy in the corner is freaking me out a little, though."

Travis peered over his shoulder to the man seated on a black chaise. The stranger had been staring at her on and off for the last hour. Every time she glanced up, his gaze was focused on her, his hand on his boxer-covered erection.

Travis turned back to her. "I can get Leo to make him stop."

"No." She shook her head. God, no.

All she wanted was to get through the remainder of her

shift without seeing her boss at all. She owed him an apology, but she wasn't in the right mood to give it at the moment. "It's fine. I noticed another woman doing the exact same thing to you earlier. If it's normal, I can deal." At least for the next hour until her shift was over, then she'd go home, scrub her skin until she no longer felt dirty and drown her sorrows with chocolate.

The tops of Travis's cheeks darkened.

"Are you blushing?" She grinned.

"That was Melissa." He broke eye contact, busying himself with wiping down the already clean counter. "She gets off on people watching her get off."

*And he loves it.*

"But I'm used to it," he added. "If that guy makes you feel uncomfortable, just say so."

She shook her head dismissively and glanced past the man in the corner one more time. No matter how ripped the guy's abs were or how sexy his jaw line, he still made her skin crawl. Only dealing with Leo wasn't an option. She'd have to ignore the sleazy masturbation stare.

"So give me a rundown of the rules." She needed a distraction. "How does someone get access to this part of the club? And why do I rarely see people entering from upstairs?"

"There's a long list of rules." Travis threw his dishcloth into the sink and moved to lean against the counter beside her. "The club isn't advertised. It runs merely on word of mouth and is only open on Saturday nights. Anyone who wants to attend has to pass guidelines set by T.J., Leo, and Brute."

"Guidelines?"

"Haven't you noticed that most of the guys are ripped?"

Shay frowned and scanned the patrons. He was right. There wasn't an overweight man in sight. They were all reasonably athletic, some more so than others.

"Men have to be to a certain standard—physically fit, no love handles. I think there's even a rule on chest and back hair."

"And how is it policed? They walk through the club, bare their chest and can't get access if they're too hairy or overweight?"

Travis chuckled. "An application has to be submitted via email every time someone wants to join the fun. Men have to attach an image of themselves in nothing but their underwear. And women have to provide a headshot. If they don't fit the criteria, they don't gain entry, and if the photos they send are bogus, either the security guards will turn them away at the door, or whoever is on duty down here will have a quiet word with them."

"And what's with the different standards?" Shay was all for women's rights, but most of the females down here weren't held to the same standard as the men. There were a lot of curves and full breasts jiggling around. "How come women don't have to meet the same criteria?"

"Would you fuck a fat and hairy guy?"

Shay winced. "I guess I never really thought about it." She wasn't into hairy men, but if Wolverine found his way into her bed, she sure as shit wouldn't kick him out. Yet, she had to admit, she'd never been with a man with weight issues.

"See? Women are more selective than men. Everyone pays a hefty price to enter the doors. So, Brute vets applications and selects guests based on who is more likely to interact better with others. Guys tend to want to get naked with any woman with a good dose of confidence and sexuality, no matter what size, shape or color."

Travis grabbed a tall glass from the dishwasher rack, scooped in some ice and filled it with water from the soda dispenser. "We have couples' night, where most attendants are in a long-term relationship but want to play with other likeminded couples. Ladies' night has a ratio sixty-percent female, to forty-percent male, and vice-versa for people looking for more man action."

Shay's mind buzzed from the onslaught of debauchery. "Wow. I'm blown away, not only at being in a fully functioning sex club, but the amount of detail the guys have put into it."

Travis smirked. "*Blown* away?"

She rolled her eyes at the innuendo and nudged his shoulder. "I guess I had that one coming to me."

He snorted, showing a dazzling smile. He was an attractive guy, clean shaven, nice build, light-green eyes against his smooth, dark skin. No wonder women stared at him while they rowed the boat. He was capable of inspiring scream-worthy orgasms from his looks alone.

"Do you ever play?" She broke eye contact as the question fell like a stone between them. It wasn't a pickup line, yet it sounded like it once the words left her lips.

"The more you work down here, the more open-minded you become. I suppose it's only natural that staff are allowed to participate on their nights off, or after the last call for drinks."

"You didn't answer my question." She gave his shoulder another nudge.

"Oh, you noticed that, did you?" He placed the glass of water against his lips and slowly sipped.

Hint taken. "How about the owners? Do the same rules apply for T.J. and Brute?" And Leo, she added silently.

The jealousy from earlier hadn't faded. She still pictured the man of her dreams caressing another woman, staring at her longingly. Please tell me management have their own set of rules where they can't participate.

"Do you really want to hear the answer?" He placed his glass on the counter and looked her in the eye. "You've got a thing for Leo."

It wasn't a question, so she didn't bother answering.

"He's active, Shay." His eyes softened as he spoke. "They all spend a lot of time down here."

Damn.

That hurt more than she'd anticipated. She nodded, breaking eye contact. It was over then—her infatuation, the flirting, the heart-fluttering moments she always hoped would turn into something more.

As if called from her thoughts, Leo appeared at the doorway of one of the rooms. His gaze sought hers, and before she could look away, he broke the connection and moved into the next room.

Shit.

She didn't even have the upper hand with glance-aways. This sucked...harder than the woman in the corner making slurping sounds around a bodybuilder's cock.

She couldn't stop the throbbing ache in her chest from intensifying. It hurt to think of him with other women. Not only because she was jealous, but because she genuinely liked him. Leo was a great guy, sex-club tendencies or not. He held a certain charm she'd never seen before. She'd even go as far to say he was a true gentleman under the layers of arrogance, stubbornness and the inability to believe he was ever wrong.

Shay was thankful when a guy wearing silk boxers sidled up to the bar, dispersing her pity party. With a silent jut of his chin to Travis, he turned his back and concentrated on the threesome taking place in front of the mega porn screen.

"He's a regular," Travis murmured. "He'll probably be here next week. Always orders bourbon on the rocks."

She acknowledged the drink with a nod, but her gaze kept drifting back to the room Leo had entered. Her insides were being torn apart, one side of her wanting to know what he was doing, the other not willing to find out.

"Where's the bathroom," she spoke above a whisper. She

needed a live-porn breather, to get the sounds, the scent and the images out of her mind. At least for a little while.

"First door to the left." He pointed a lazy hand to one of the open doorways. "At the end of the room, there are female and male amenities with showers and anything else you or any of the patrons should need."

Shay frowned. What the hell did that mean? "Okay. I'll be back in a minute."

"You should call it a night." Travis slid the drink along the bar to silk-boxers guy, and met her gaze. "You're starting to look pale, and your shift is almost over anyway. Go home and regroup before next weekend."

Shay let out a sigh. The guy she liked was a deviant, she didn't know how she could continue working at the job she loved, and now she apparently looked like shit. "Yeah. I might do that." She continued to the first room on the left, staring at her toes, concentrating on each footstep so she didn't falter and draw unwanted attention.

When she reached the doorway, a shiver of apprehension ran over her skin. This room was quiet, no orgasmic banshee calls or heated moans, just the faint sound of a female giggle and the deep murmurings of more than one male.

Curiosity grabbed hold of her ovaries and held tight until she raised her gaze to the three people on the lone bed in the room. Comfy-looking sofas and ottomans lined the walls, but the main focal point was the bed, illuminated by tiny lights in the ceiling. A curvy blonde reclined in the center, her face bright with a beautiful smile, her body entirely naked, her thighs slightly parted to expose her smooth sex.

A man lay on her right, propped on one elbow, his gaze focused on the woman with adoration while he idly drew trails around the smooth skin of her hip with his fingers. On her left lay another, his head bowed to her chest. It wasn't until Shay took another step that she could see him placing delicate kisses around the side of the woman's breast.

Shay held her breath, overcome with an emotion she couldn't pinpoint. Envy? Distaste? The scene before her was mesmerizing. The gentle way the men paid attention to the beaming woman. The way their cocks stood hard as stone, yet they weren't rutting on their prize like a dog in heat. It seemed almost romantic... In a sex club? Holy fuck, Shay was confused.

"Hey." The man facing her greeted with a genuine smile.

The connection was enough to make her footsteps falter. "Ah. Hi."

She wasn't familiar with the protocol of sex-club conversation. What was she supposed to say? How's it hanging...when clearly it wasn't hanging at all.

She lowered her gaze with a frown and increased her pace to the bathroom. Once inside, she pushed the door shut and leaned against the wall beside it, breathing deep to control her anxiety.

This was ridiculous. She was a strong, self-assured, grown woman. Not a fumbling, blubbering mess. This shit had to stop. Only she didn't know how to curb the unfamiliar flutter of butterflies in her belly, or shake the sordid thoughts in her mind.

Going back to her main bar job and acting normal was going to require an Oscar-winning performance. She wouldn't be able to look T.J., Brute or Leo in the eye again. Not without picturing them entangled in a mass orgy of beautiful people. And it pissed her off even more when her pussy began to tingle at the image.

She usually owned her sexuality. Getting herself off wasn't something she was embarrassed about. She had toys, watched porn and had the occasional one-night stand. But this...a sex club, was way beyond her depths. Travis was right. Going home early was the best option.

And what the hell was on the vanity? She straightened and made her way to the basin, ignoring her reflection in the mirror. Along the ceramic counter stood a myriad of deodorant bottles, all different brands placed neatly in a line. Beside them were bath towels, plush and dark with some already discarded in the thick wicker basket beside the vanity. In front of the towels was a laminated list of rules taped to the counter. Her management trio really had thought of everything. The page listed privacy requirements, the need for regular STD checks, instructions on washing after every play session, right down to the necessity to place condoms on sex toys before use.

She groaned, reaffirmed in her decision to leave. Her brain was fried, and every compiling aspect made her overreact. She turned, about to flee, when the door swooshed open and the attractive blonde from the bed walked in.

"Are you all right?" The woman stood before Shay with a whole heap of exposed tits and pussy.

With no control to stop it, Shay's gaze raked the woman's body, over the hardened nipples, the glint of jewelry in her navel, the crevices of bare vagina, to the smooth thighs and finally her dark painted toe nails.

*Awkward. Stare at those toes. Do not take your focus away from those fucking toes.*

"Umm." Shay cleared her throat. "I'm fine."

"Do you mind handing me a towel?"

Shay was thankful for the excuse to turn her back, and gave the woman what she wanted.

"Is that better?"

Shay raised her gaze to the woman now covered in the large towel, feeling a slight reprieve to the massive case of holy-fuck-get-me-out-of-here. "Thanks," she murmured, ignoring the heat climbing up her neck.

"Now tell me what's really wrong."

Shay frowned.

"Come on." The woman strolled past her and jumped to sit on the vanity counter. "Spill. You look like you're caught between disgust and shock."

Ouch. "Is it that obvious?"

The woman nodded. "Kinda. I've been around the club for a while. I've seen a lot of virgins walk through the doors."

"Oh, I'm no virgin." Shay shook her head. The situation continued to worsen. Not only was her distaste evident, but she was acting so childish people thought she was pure.

"Sex-club virgin, honey." She chuckled. "It's nothing to worry about. You just look out of place."

The clarification didn't help. "I don't think I'm cut out for this type of scene. Even as a working environment."

"Why are you apprehensive?"

Shay didn't know where to start. The list in her mind seemed a mile long and it was all exacerbated because the man she liked was a participant and the owner. "It's...so..." She shrugged. She didn't know this woman, and she certainly didn't want to offend her any more than she probably already had.

"Would it help if I told you why I come here?"

The woman focused on Shay with genuine concern, like they were best friends trying to get through a challenging situation. There was no reason for it, but Shay felt a slight connection to the woman's sincerity. Maybe it was because she wanted to cling to the only person who didn't currently have exposed assets.

"I guess."

"I'm single." The woman grinned, as if her status was a badge of honor. "I work. Hard. Every damn day, and at the end of the week, I want someone to snuggle up to. My job doesn't give me time to date, and I don't really want that drama in my life at the moment. But what I do want is a little attention every now and then."

The woman paused, waiting for a reaction. Shay could only nod in acknowledgement.

"I love sex." The woman's smile widened. "However, men can be selfish assholes."

Shay released a soft chuckle. "You're preaching to the choir."

"I guess it's hard to explain. And I suppose, even harder for an outsider to understand. But down here, it's like family." The woman cringed. "Wow. That came out wrong."

Shay snorted with delirium and came to rest against the vanity, listening intently.

"Everyone down here wants sex. And I guess, because we are all somewhat assured of getting what we crave, people are more giving. The guys..." her eyes glittered, "...they are ah-may-zing. If you say no they immediately back off. There are no questions, no recriminations, no judgments."

It sounded amazing, in theory. "But don't you feel weird having a crowd of people watch you?"

"Have you ever been watched?" The woman raised a brow. "Have you ever fantasized about someone watching you?"

"Maybe." Shay shrugged and felt the heat crawl back up her neck when the woman grinned.

"It's a rush. And most of all, for me, it's uplifting. Knowing another man, or woman, is aroused because of what you're doing." The woman crossed her legs, making the towel rise up her thighs. "Security is also a big bonus. I come here knowing I won't be assaulted or abused. I don't have to seduce men and risk my safety by leaving a public place with them or taking them back to my home, which is secluded and would make me vulnerable. For me, there's no other

43

option, until I want to settle down and focus on finding a husband."

Shay broke eye contact and stared at the polished tiled floor. It made sense. Picking up men involved risk and wasn't usually worth the effort.

"I'm Zoe by the way."

"Shay."

"Well, Shay, I know you're down here as a staff member, not a participant, but try and look at the club without reservations. Imagine what it would be like if two guys were smothering you with affection, their sole focus on your pleasure."

The fantasy heated her nipples and she crossed her arms over her chest in frustration. "I'm not looking for more than one partner."

"That's understandable. And I bet you already have someone in mind." Zoe quirked her sultry lips. "Rumors are already spreading about Leo commanding you aren't to be touched. He's a great guy. You'd be a lucky woman if you gained his long-term interest."

No luck there. Shay was far from gaining his interest.

"He's a sexual man, though. You'd need to get over your inhibitions."

Shay released a heavy breath, unsure if getting over her inhibitions was an option. Or even worth it. From Leo, she wanted love. And it didn't seem possible to establish a relationship in this environment.

A loud bang sounded on the door and Shay startled. "Shit."

"Shay, are you in there?" Leo's voice boomed from outside the bathroom.

"Wow." Zoe pushed off the counter. "The boss sounds like he's going caveman on your ass. Do you really want to miss the opportunity to have all that raw masculinity to yourself?"

"But that's just it—" She wanted to discuss her issues concerning monogamy but another loud knock cut her off.

"*Shay.*"

"I'll leave you to it." Zoe unwrapped the towel from around her body and placed it in the wicker basket. "I have two very lovely men to get back to."

Shay straightened and had to stop herself from begging the woman not to leave. She didn't want to be left alone with Leo. So far tonight, all they'd done was argue. She wanted to go back to the flirting and fun, the innuendo and batting eyelashes, and forget this discovery had ever been made.

Instead, she swallowed the nausea creeping up her throat and rubbed at the rampant butterflies in her belly. "Thank you."

"No problem, honey. Come find me if you ever have any questions."

Shay gripped the counter behind her, oblivious to the naked curves strutting from the bathroom, and focused on the man who reached to hold open the door. She'd never seen Leo so furious. His eyes were narrowed slits, his jaw tight, his hands clenched in fists at his side while wild strands of hair shadowed his features.

"What's going on?" His harsh tone hit harder than the current glare he fixed her with.

She could understand his aggression. She'd insulted him earlier and it would take more than a few hours for him to get over it. An apology was necessary. She just couldn't find the strength to say it. Not tonight. Not when her heart was bleeding and her temples throbbing.

"I'm going to the bathroom." She pulled a face. *Duh.*

"Cut the crap, Shay. You've been in here for fifteen minutes." He strode inside the women's bathroom like his shit was red hot and let the door fall closed behind him. "Are you capable of working the bar next weekend or not?"

She straightened, taking his question as a fresh insult to her capabilities. "Of course I am. You know that."

"Do I? You made it clear you don't approve of the scene. I don't want you spreading hate toward the patrons. They pay good money to be here."

*Fuck you.*

She returned his glare. "I'd never do that." And besides, she didn't have hate to spread. Every passing minute made her realize her aversion was from being clueless about the lifestyle. For singles, it seemed like the perfect way to have fun. She didn't know if she'd ever try it herself or understand the reasons why someone in a committed relationship would join, but her horizons were inching a tiny bit wider.

"Really?" He shrugged. "I guess I don't know what to expect from you anymore."

"From me? Are you kidding?" She raised her voice. "*You* blindsided *me*, remember? You knew I had feelings for you, and you strung me along like a lost puppy. And all this time I never had a chance."

"Because I knew you'd act like this," he snarled. "This is who I am, Shay, and I knew you'd never want a part of it." He stepped forward, closing in on her. "I didn't lead you on. I tried my fucking hardest to stay away. Do you think I haven't imagined spreading your thighs a thousand damn times since you started working here? Or wondered what it would be like if you enjoyed the club scene. I've been living in my own private hell, unable to stop you from dragging me round by the dick."

His angered breaths brushed her lips as her mouth dried.

"You never gave me a chance." She swallowed over the gravel in her throat. He didn't have the right to make assumptions about her sexuality, just like she hadn't had the right to insult him earlier.

"I did." His voice lowered to a whisper. "Months ago, when I touched you in the storeroom."

Shay narrowed her gaze on his ocean eyes. "I don't understand."

"I was testing you. Once and for all, I needed to know how you reacted to sex. If you'd be open-minded enough to try things out of your comfort zone. Yet, even in the privacy of a storeroom, you acted shocked and distraught at what we'd done."

No. Fucking. Way. She blinked at him, not sure whether to set him straight or claw his eyes out. "I wasn't distraught."

She'd been shocked, yes, because it was the first time a guy had unselfishly pleasured her. Usually, she was the one giving sexual favors without her own gratification. She'd been flustered, trying to hide her growing infatuation and adoration because he'd treated her the way she'd always wanted to be treated. In that moment, her feelings had passed the point of infatuation and she'd struggled to disguise it.

"You should've given me the opportunity to make my own decisions." She stepped to the side, needing space from his cloying dominance. "I might have tried."

He bridged the gap between them, hovering over her. "Prove it."

"Prove what?" She shuddered, trying to ignore the throb beginning to pulse in her pussy.

He took another step, backing her into the counter, bringing them thigh to thigh. "That you'd try." His gaze was bleak as he pressed the hardness of his erection against her abdomen. "Try for me. Now," he whispered.

She shook her head. Not tonight. Not when her heart was barely beating and her mind couldn't control her rampant thoughts. He didn't deserve it. Nor did she. No matter how much her pussy throbbed in encouragement. "No."

Slowly, he leaned forward, his light dusting of stubble brushing her cheek. She shivered, her thoughts and body swaying as he murmured in her ear.

"Your lips say no, but your body says otherwise. Which is it?"

She closed her eyes, unable to decide, unable to breathe. She ran her hand around his neck for grounding and prayed the right choice would hurry up and make itself known. All she'd ever wanted was his attention, his desire, but the timing and her insecurities were tainting the X-rated fairytale she'd imagined.

"Shay." Her name was a whisper against her neck as he brought one of his hands to rest on the counter, the other on her hip, and then slowly moved upward. "Please don't torture me."

Him?

He'd been endlessly tormenting her for longer than she could remember. "I don't know what to do."

Her body was on fire, her nipples hard, her sex fluttering. But people were on the other side of that door. Naked people. Anyone could walk in. Anyone could see them and think their intimacy was a show to be watched. Did that matter? Right now, she had no fucking clue. The heat of his body made it hard to rationalize.

He parted her legs with his knee and ground the hardness of his thigh against her mound. Her sex creamed in response, bursting to life in a mass of tingles. Damn her treacherous body.

A whimper escaped her throat and she clung tighter to his neck. She wanted him so much it hurt, but she didn't want to hate herself afterward. If she did this, it needed to be for the right reasons. And all of her had to be onboard—mind, body and soul. Not just her pussy.

"I can't." She released him and placed her hands against his chest. "I need more time."

He stiffened, killing her slowly in the following silent seconds. "Okay." He stepped back, keeping his focus lowered. The hard length of his erection strained against the crotch of his pants, and it suddenly hit her that he might go elsewhere for relief.

"It's almost time for you to knock off anyway. You may as well go home and get the extra sleep."

Alarm bells rang in her ears. His instant dismissal only exacerbated her theory of him taking another woman. Her stomach nose-dived, freefalling while she silently sucked in a deep breath. The distress must have been written on her face, because when he glanced up, his features softened.

"I don't want to hurt you."

"But you will, right?" she choked. "I'll drive away the same moment you drive your dick into someone else."

She instantly regretted the words, even before the look of loathing crossed his face. Calm under pressure, she was not.

"I'm not a fucking animal," he spoke through clenched teeth and spun away from her, heading for the door. "Go home, Shay."

# CHAPTER FIVE

*L*eo slid onto one of the bar stools and kept his head lowered, his hands fisted into tight balls below the counter. He was on the cusp of losing his shit. He'd never been this angry in his life. His heart was pounding, his head throbbing, and if he clenched his teeth any tighter, he was sure he'd crack a tooth.

"Scotch," he barked at Travis.

Shay continued to come out swinging, and he only had himself to blame. He was the reason she was acting like a wounded animal backed into a corner. He should've waited until she came out of the bathroom, into the open, instead of storming in on her. Only he hadn't been able to curb his worry when he couldn't find her behind the bar. He let panic choose his actions instead of common sense, and yet again, he was nursing wounded pride.

"Here you go, boss."

Leo grasped the glass that slid in front of him and downed it in two burning gulps. Sweet Jesus, that stung. He wanted to order another, to get shit-faced and bury his troubles in the depths of another woman's body just to piss Shay off. It wouldn't take much for him to be the asshole she thought he was. But no matter how angry he became, he wouldn't stoop that low.

He had a heart. And although he wanted to, he couldn't blame Shay for her backhanded comments. She was in shock and always flew off the handle when she didn't have tight control of her emotions. He'd seen it happen too many times to count. It was one of her not-so-endearing charms—the way she showed she was hurting by shooting out a rapid, uncensored response.

"I'm going home." Her voice broke his thoughts.

He held tight to his glass, trying hard not to raise his gaze. She wasn't speaking to him anyway. From his periphery, he watched her grab her cell from the counter and shove it in her pocket. "I hope to see you again, Travis."

"You too, Sas-Shay."

*Quit the endearments, Travis, or I'll break your face.*

She strode back around the counter, not acknowledging Leo's existence, not bothering with a see you later, asshole, and stormed away. The need to chase after her clawed at his back. He even had to fight not to glance over his shoulder and watch her leave.

"Fuck that."

He'd walked down this shitty path before. He was stronger than this. She was only a woman, after all. Nobody should have a tight rein on his dick like she did. Then again, she'd always been more than a typical woman to him. He'd been attracted to her since the day she'd handed in her employment application.

Tempting looks aside, he was drawn to her for too many reasons. She worked hard, played even harder, and owned her independence. She didn't placate others and never hid behind a fake façade. He needed a strong-willed woman like that. He needed her, period.

"Want to talk about it?" Travis asked.

Leo raised his gaze and glared.

The bartender held up his hands in surrender. "I guess not." He began polishing the beer taps. "Let me know when you cool down. I need to speak to you about a minor issue with Shay earlier."

Issue? As if he wasn't going to bite at that statement. "What issue?"

"It isn't major, and she didn't want me to make a big deal about it." He shrugged. "Glenn kept staring at her from the corner while he jerked off. I don't think she was prepared for that sort of thing. It freaked her out."

Of course she wasn't fucking prepared. Leo hadn't given her the time to be. He'd crumpled under Brute and T.J.'s suggestion, not wanting to out his infatuation for her and completely cocked up the situation. He pushed from his stool, ready to...he didn't know what, and stepped back into a human wall.

"It's just me," T.J. spoke from behind him. "Where's Shay?"

"Shh," Leo snapped and raised his brows at Travis to continue.

"There was no issue," he reiterated. "She was cool about it and made it clear she didn't want anything said to you or Glenn. But I thought I'd let you know, I had a quiet word with him anyway. I told him tonight was her first night and she was a little skittish."

"Fuck." Leo huffed out a breath and rubbed his forehead. "We're going to lose our best bartender." He was going to lose her. "Shay's out of her fucking mind." He rounded on T.J. "And it's all your fault."

He ignored his friend's frown of annoyance and scoped the room. "Where is he? I want to speak to him."

"I dunno," Travis answered. "Maybe he left. Everything

was fine, though. Glenn was apologetic. He didn't realize she was new."

"Well, he should've fucking realized." Leo hoped to hell Glenn had gone home, otherwise the target of his frustrations would wish he'd never showed up tonight.

"Calm down," T.J. muttered. "Travis took care of it."

But what about Shay? Who was taking care of her?

Leo slumped back onto the bar stool. "Tonight was a total fuck up."

"Why?" T.J. asked. "Couldn't she hack it?"

"I thought she did a great job," Travis added.

Leo glanced over his shoulder at T.J., not bothering to hide the vulnerability itching to break free. "No." He shook his head. "It didn't go well. I'm not sure if she'll come back." To the club, or back into his life. And after all the women who'd dismissed him due to his sexual proclivities, Shay's rejection was by far the worst to take.

~

Shay fled up the staircase and rushed through the Shot of Sin dance crowd. Without a word to her bar staff, she snatched her handbag from the main bar storeroom and headed for the entrance of the club. She needed to blow this pop stand. Fast. Her chest was throbbing with regret, a sensation she was too familiar with but unfortunately couldn't control because of her shitty temper.

It was her one downfall. She couldn't hide her emotions. It was either blow up or tear up, and she fucking hated crying. But she would apologize. She always did. All she needed was a little time to ditch the fuzzy, blindsided sensation, then she'd make amends.

Once she sucked in a few deep breaths of clean, night air, she would calm down. The hope of relaxation almost had her running through the crowded entry hall to the lights illuminating the street outside.

"Leaving so soon?" Brute stepped away from the small group of females and blocked her path. His gaze narrowed, the slightest hint of concern tightening his brows. "You look ticked."

"I am ticked." Deep breath. Deep breath. "You could've warned me."

He shrugged a shoulder. "I did. I told you to stay away from Leo months ago. You didn't listen."

What?

"Was tonight about proving a point?" Her eyes burned with humiliation. "Was Leo in on this?"

"No on both counts. Tonight was about filling in for Tracy. But I admit it was an added bonus that I didn't have to spell out why the two of you aren't compatible."

Shay let out an angry breath. "Nice, Brute. Real nice." She shook her head and stepped around him.

"I care about you. We all do."

His admission made her halt. She kept her gaze on the street light beckoning her to flee. Defeat had firmly set in. She'd been humiliated, devalued and heartbroken, all in one night. And the worst part was the waning hold she had on her confidence.

"Believe me, Shay, if you two had any chance of being together, I'd be the first in line to give my congratulations. But it's not going to happen. Leo doesn't do normal. None of us do."

She released a derisive laugh. "I never knew being normal was such a repulsive attribute. I suppose I should thank you for the reality check." She turned to him with a raise brow and a fake smile. There was still no emotion to his features, no comforting smile, no pleading eyes. "Good night, Brute."

She strode away, trying to rebuild her broken walls. This

wasn't the end of the world. It was only the death of an infatuation. It didn't change the love she had for her job. It didn't make her less of a person because she hadn't experienced the joys of communal fucking. All she had to do was go home, pull on her big-girl panties and spend some time online looking at Gandy candy. Mr. David Gandy would fix everything. He always did.

The cool night air comforted her as she stepped outside, not bothering to acknowledge the bouncers standing at the door.

"You need an escort?" one of them called.

She shook her head, unable to speak. They usually made sure she reached her car safely, but she didn't want the company tonight. The two-minute walk to the staff parking lot at the back of the building wasn't going to kill her.

She needed to get home. And the sooner the better. The thin material of her figure-hugging top was making her skin crawl. Even the light breeze against her cheeks was beginning to make her whimper.

What a fucking disaster.

Turning the corner, she slowed her pace, needing to calm herself before sliding behind the wheel.

"Hey, miss."

Her gaze snapped around at the deep voice. Oh, shit. It was the guy from Vault of Sin, the one who'd thought she was God's gift to masturbation. She ignored him and increased her pace. Adrenaline spurred her faster, her legs almost breaking into a run.

"I just want to talk."

In a darkened parking lot? In the early hours of the morning? After jerking off in front of her?

No thanks.

"I'm not interested." She palmed her keys, ready for anything. Everything.

Turning the far corner of the building, she chanced another glance over her shoulder and stumbled across the loose asphalt. Her bag slid from her shoulder, falling to the ground, and the spike of fear almost had her doubling over.

With a squeal, she yanked the handbag strap from the ground and began to run to her car. She fumbled with the button in her hand, finally unlocking the doors as she reached for the handle. He was right behind her, she could feel it. Her senses were on red alert, waiting for a rough hand to grab her.

She yanked the door open, jumped inside and pressed the lock as fast as she could. Her hands shook trying to get the key in the ignition, and she almost sobbed in relief when they slid into place. Without pause, she gunned the engine, yanked her gearstick into reverse and floored it.

God help anyone behind me.

As she pulled out, she caught the shadow of the man standing at the corner of the building, one hand raised, asking her to stop. Okay, so maybe he wasn't right behind her, but he had more chance getting a blowjob from one of the alley cats than he did of her hitting the brakes.

Buh bye, asshole.

She watched him jog after her car from the rear-view mirror, following her to the front of the building. Pressing harder on the accelerator, she pulled onto the road, thankful for no oncoming traffic.

Two blocks down the road, she was still breathing heavy, her heart gradually descending from her throat. What a douche. Mr. Masturbator was the perfect ending to an equally perfect day. There wasn't a hope in hell she would sleep tonight, or the rest of the week for that matter. She would dread seeing Leo on Tuesday when she worked the lunch shift at the Taste of Sin restaurant. Even if she did regain her confidence, it would take a lot of effort to hide her wounded pride.

Flicking on her indicator, she pulled to a stop at the traffic lights and inwardly cursed her stupidity. If only she'd kept her mouth shut. Leo wasn't a jerk, he'd probably had no intention of sleeping with anyone tonight...until she'd overreacted and driven him to it. And who knew, in the light of day she might've been able to understand what the whole sex-club thing was about.

She wasn't a prude. Her mind was as open as a hooker's thighs. He'd shocked her, that's all. She'd never seen him with another woman, and having the mental image of him diddling the masses was heart shattering.

"Stupid. Stupid. Stupid."

She blinked back the sting in her eyes and winced when the lights from a car behind her entered her rear-vision mirror. They flashed their high beams and she glanced up to confirm the traffic lights hadn't changed.

"Nope," she muttered. "What's your problem?"

Focusing back on her mirror, her skin prickled as she zeroed in on the car behind her. No way. It was the guy from the parking lot. He'd followed her.

"Son of a bitch."

He opened his car door and her heart stopped in fear. She had no intention of sticking around. She checked for traffic and then turned through the red light, reaching for her bag as she pulled onto the main road.

He was going to follow her home and then rape and murder her. Holy shit, she was going to die. She riffled through her bag for her phone and unlocked the screen as she drove. Calling Leo wasn't an option. He already thought she was weak, and she wouldn't give him the satisfaction of rubbing it in. Instead, she clicked on T.J.'s contact and bit her lip as the phone rang.

"Hey, Shay, what's up?"

Flashing lights glared at her through the rear-view mirror,

and she whimpered. "Please help me. A guy from the club came after me in the parking lot. He's following me home. I don't know what to do."

"Baby, calm down." Concern laced his words. "Where are you?"

"I'm on the main road, a few blocks from work, heading toward the city."

"Can you turn around and come back?"

She shook her head and puffed out an anxious breath. "I don't want to take a side street and risk him running me off the road. Please, T.J., I don't know what to do."

"Don't worry, I'm coming after you. Stay on the main road and slow down so I can catch up. But don't stop. I'll be there in a minute."

"Okay." Her voice waivered. She lifted her foot off the accelerator, slowing the car well below the speed limit. The guy behind her continued to flash his lights, his arm now waving out the window, his finger pointing to the side of the road.

This was karma. She'd been a raging bitch to Leo, and now she was paying the price. Either her stalker was going to ram into her car and drag her out the door, or she'd have a heart attack while she waited.

*Chill.*

She sucked in a shaky breath, let it out slowly and turned on the radio. The lethargic, early morning music did nothing to soothe her. All she could do was continue to hyperventilate and wait.

As she reached a yield sign, a horn blasted, startling her. A car sped up beside her on the wrong side of the road, and Leo's face stared at her from the passenger window. Shit. She didn't know if she should be relieved or more frightened from the heat in his eyes.

"Pull over," he mouthed, his lips set in a solemn line.

She did as instructed, driving through the intersection and pulling to the curb in front of the next street light. T.J.'s car parked behind her, and the other guy followed. Before she had time to cut the engine, she saw Leo in her rear-view mirror. He flung open his door and climbed from the car with his shoulders broad with menace. There wasn't an ounce of softness to his features as he turned his back and jogged to the stranger's car.

"Oh, shit." She watched in horror as he yanked the guy out by his shirt and thrust him against the side of the vehicle.

"Shay."

She screamed and then clasped a hand over her mouth. T.J. stood outside her car, one hand on the door handle while the other tapped on her window until she released the lock. He opened the door as she unclicked her seatbelt and then reached down to help her out.

"Come here."

She could hear Leo yelling as she went willingly into T.J.'s arms.

"It was just a misunderstanding," he cooed in her ear.

Misunderstanding?

She tilted her head, listening to Leo verbally abuse the man. "Well, you don't fucking chase after her. You drop the keys with the bouncers and let her figure out she's lost them. Why did you follow her into the parking lot anyway?"

Keys?

"Travis came to me in the club and said I freaked her out. I felt like shit and wanted to apologize." The man was almost talking too fast for her to understand, yet, all the awkward pieces began falling into place. "I gathered I was scaring her, so I stopped following, but she dropped her handbag and didn't pick up her keys. I'm sorry. It was my initial reaction to go after her."

Shay winced. "I'm such a tool."

"No, you're not." T.J. hugged her tight. "He should've known better than to go after you. You had every reason to be frightened."

She whimpered and closed her eyes, resting her head against his shoulder. The jingle of keys sounded and then a car door slammed. She closed her lids tighter as the stranger's car sped off and heavy footsteps approached.

When the crunch against the asphalt stopped, she held her breath in the silence. She couldn't look at Leo, couldn't take the anger in his eyes or the annoyance at her stupidity. Instead, she burrowed deeper into T.J., hoping he'd hold her a little longer, until she recovered enough from her embarrassment to drive home.

"I'll take it from here," Leo spoke softly.

Her lids fluttered open and her lips trembled with the need to protest as T.J. retreated a step. He gave a sad smile and stroked a lazy hand through her hair. "I'll head back to the club and close things up for the night. Call me if you need anything."

*No. Don't leave me.*

She stared wide-eyed, silently begging him not to bail on her. Especially when Leo didn't look like he was going anywhere. "I'll be fine," she croaked, hoping the two of them would leave together. "Thank you both." She kept her focus on T.J., no matter how hard Leo's gaze bore into the side of her face. "I'll see you both next week."

T.J. waited, scrutinizing her.

"I said I'd take care of it," Leo growled. "Just go."

A shiver ran down her spine at his command, and she twisted around to her car, ready to flee. She pulled open the door to the sound of T.J.'s retreating steps, then the air left her lungs as a heavy hand wove around her waist and slammed it shut again.

He was right behind her, his chest at her back, his breath

in her hair. "I'll drive you home," he murmured, making her come undone, dragging the uncontrollable emotions higher up her throat.

She shook her head. They'd fought enough tonight. The battle scars still stung across her heart. Being around him now would make it ten times harder to stop the tears she despised from flowing. She wasn't a fucking crier. The last time she'd shed tears was years ago. And she'd be damned if she broke the achievement by blubbering over an enthusiastic masturbator and a case of mistaken intentions.

"I'm a big girl. I can drive myself home." She stood rigid, waiting for him to back off, hoping the warmth sinking under her skin would quickly vanish.

"Please, Shay."

His plea undid her. He didn't say another word, just continued to lean into her, his breath fanning her neck, his scent driving her crazy as T.J. pulled out from behind them. Leo placed his hand on her hip, sending a shudder through her stomach and higher to her nipples. She closed her eyes again, wishing the darkness would give her strength. But it didn't, it only gave her the image of him in her mind, the light dusting of stubble, the tempting lips she'd fall to her knees to taste.

She couldn't take it any longer, couldn't find the strength she hoped beyond hope to find. She turned in his arms, leaned against the cold metal of the car and stared up at him. Fragility stared back at her. His eyes were now a darker shade of blue, his forehead creased with a slight frown.

"I'm sorry," she whispered.

There, she'd apologized, so why did she still feel terrible?

"It's not your fault. Glenn knows better than to approach someone outside the club, no matter what the circumstances."

"No." She shook her head and lowered her gaze to the

tanned skin exposed above the top button of his shirt. "I'm sorry for being such a bitch."

"Don't be." His response was immediate, without reservation.

Her guilt increased at his sudden acceptance of her apology.

"Your sexuality is none of my business," she continued. She deserved his wrath, and getting it over and done with now would make it easier to return to work next week.

"I kinda made it your business." The side of his lips tilted in a sly grin.

"It still doesn't excuse the way I acted."

"No, it doesn't." Seriousness entered his features. "But as your boss, I should've prepared you better. And—don't roll your eyes at me—because we're friends, I should've prepared you better. I'm not letting you get away with being a bitch. I'm just saying that I know you, and I should've expected the jabs at my ego. It's what you do when you're upset."

"You don't know me that well," she retorted. He didn't know her at all if he thought her side of their relationship was based on mere friendship. "I thought I knew you too..." She let the sentence hang.

"You do know me, Shay." He placed his hands on her hips, holding her tight, bringing them pelvis to hard, unyielding pelvis. "There's just one tiny aspect of my life you didn't know about."

"Tiny aspect?" She wanted to snort. A hidden tattoo equated to a tiny aspect. Owning and participating in a sex club was such an enormous part of his life that it deserved its own zip code.

"My sex life doesn't define me. I'm still the guy..."

She quirked a brow. Did he really not know how she felt? Or did saying it aloud make him uncomfortable?

"I fell in love with?" she answered for him. She was too

tired for games, and maybe exposing how she felt would make him understand why Vault of Sin had rocked her foundations so hard. It wasn't all the cock swinging around, or all the screaming, squealing and grunting. It was the loss of love she now knew would never be returned.

Leo stared at her with narrowing eyes.

Yeah, asshole. Those overreactions were because of love, not my so-called normalness.

"I need to get home." She turned away from his scrutiny. "I'll drop you back at the club."

"No."

He grabbed her hand and led her to the other side of the car. She was helpless, her body craving his touch so much she didn't protest when he opened the passenger-side door and waited for her to climb in. As she clasped her belt, he loomed over her, his focus growing with intent.

"I'll get you home. Hopefully by then I'll have some semblance of mental capacity after the bomb you just dropped. Then I'll make us some coffee, 'cause we sure as shit aren't finished with this conversation."

# CHAPTER SIX

$\mathcal{L}$eo pulled into Shay's townhouse driveway, not entirely sure how he got there. He'd seen her home once before, at the end of a staff Christmas party. Tonight's trip had been done on autopilot. The drive had been silent, nothing but the churning of his brain to keep him company.

Love. Holy fuck.

Talk about a punch to the testicles. He didn't know whether to let excitement take hold, or if he should cut and run. Every woman he'd shown his true sexuality to had gutted him with their rapid rejection. And even though Shay had technically done the same, he couldn't fight the desire to let the grin pulling at his lips take hold. There was a glimmer of hope in this fucked-up mess. A glimmer he might be willing to explore, even though the pain from the past made him cautious.

Cutting the engine, he turned off the lights and sat in the darkened silence as she unbuckled her belt.

"I'm exhausted." Her fragile tone reaffirmed her words. "Can we talk about this another day? Or maybe never?"

Like hell. Love had never been within his grasp. He wouldn't let it go easily. "Sorry, little girl. We're doing this now."

Her head snapped around, her light-brown irises darkening as the side of her jaw flexed.

There you go. An added boost of adrenaline to keep you awake. He loved the way her eyes flared when he taunted her. He loved her sass. Fuck. He really did adore this woman.

She yanked her handbag from the floor, climbed from the car and slammed the door in a huff. He chuckled to himself while she stormed to the front of her home and began searching for her keys. The keys Glenn had picked up from the parking-lot asphalt and were now firmly sitting in Leo's trouser pocket.

After a few seconds of searching, she straightened and swung around to glare at him.

With a grin, he climbed from the car and jogged to her side.

"My keys?" She thrust out her palm. "*Please*."

He retrieved them from his pocket and placed them in her hand, touching her for longer than necessary. Her skin was soft, warm and too damn inviting after the anger he'd received from her earlier. As much as he liked teasing her, he hated her ire. Her lips were meant for smiling, not snarling. And he never wanted to see those light-brown irises peering up at him with anything other than lust and affection.

"Thank you," she muttered and then turned to open the door.

He followed her down a pitch-black hall and squinted when she flicked on a light to reveal an open kitchen, dining and living room area. She went to the fridge, retrieved a bottle of water and spun to him as she cracked open the lid.

"So...can we get this chat over with?" She raised a haughty

brow. She was flustered, still the frightened lioness backed into a corner.

"No need to be aggressive. All I want to do is talk."

"Aggressive? No. I'm in shock. I'm disappointed. I'm probably overreacting a little, but I'm not aggressive. I just want to go to bed."

He quirked a brow, arrogantly suggesting he join her.

"Alone, Leo."

He held in a chuckle, yet he couldn't keep the side of his lips from tilting. Her vulnerability warmed his heart, made him yearn more to protect her. "Don't worry about next week. I'll find someone else to work the shift."

"Are you kidding?" She pushed from the counter and straightened her shoulders. "Working down there isn't the problem. I don't give a flying hoot what nameless, faceless people do in their spare time. This is about you blindsiding me when I'd made it clear I had feelings for you."

"I'm sorry." Even though her reactions had sparked an avalanche of bickering, this mess between them was his fault. He should've put his foot down when T.J. suggested she work in the Vault.

"You should've told me I had no chance."

"I tried." He moved forward slowly, not wanting to spook her into running. "After the time in the storeroom, I backed away."

She slumped against the counter and stared at the floor. "You know how women play hard to get because men like a challenge?"

He frowned. "Yeah."

"It works for women, too." She shrugged. "You only made me want you more."

"I should've known." He walked into the kitchen and rested his lower back against the counter opposite her. "I'm kinda irresistible. Sometimes I forget the effect I have on the opposite sex."

She glanced at him under thick eyelashes and released a huff of laughter. "You're a dick," she muttered, shaking her head and lowering her gaze back to the floor.

Silence fell between them, giving him the time to relive the mistakes he'd made. He never should've reciprocated her flirting. He sure as hell shouldn't have succumbed to temptation and followed her into the storeroom that day. In truth, he probably shouldn't have hired her when he realized he desired her the first day they met. Now she was fractured —her skin pale, her eyes empty, her smile hiding under layers of betrayal.

She raised her hands and stared blankly at her palms.

"You're shaking." He bridged the space between them in two strides and clasped her hands in his, ignoring the way she stiffened.

"It's been a long night."

She straightened the closer he inched forward, trying to maintain space between them. After a long shift at the club, she smelled like sin. Like hot, sweaty, entirely delectable sin.

Fuck his proclivities. Why couldn't he be happy to settle down in a normal relationship? It wasn't like he couldn't function without the thrill of exhibitionism. He'd lived without it before. He hadn't been happy, but then again, he hadn't had the right woman either.

Christ. Who was he kidding? He couldn't erase parts of his soul at will. If only. Life would be so much simpler. But he was finally confident with the harsh realities of his lifestyle. He'd earned his take-it-or-leave-it mentality. He owed it to himself not to revert back to being ashamed.

"I should call a cab." He let the words fall between them but didn't move. He couldn't. Her body was so warm against his, the lush curve of her breasts within his grasp, her soft lips tilted toward him.

"Yeah. You should." She didn't pull her hands away. Didn't slide out from between his body and the counter.

Listening to his libido would be a mistake. He'd get her into bed, make love to her until the sun rose, and they'd awaken to compounded problems that neither one of them wanted to face. Only he couldn't find the strength to step back.

"Want me to stay the night?"

Her throat worked over a heavy swallow. "You shouldn't."

She stood against him, her beautiful brown eyes darkening with lust, the swell of her breasts rising and falling with such innocent seduction that his balls tightened. He was stunned by her nearness. By the fact she knew his dirty little secret and still allowed him to be this close.

He released her hands, cupped her cheek and leaned his face close to hers. "I no longer give a shit about what we should and shouldn't do. I asked you what you wanted, Shay. Nothing else matters."

She ran a nervous swipe of her tongue over her bottom lip. "I..." She frowned and shook her head. "You know how I feel about you. But I'm not looking to sleep around. I'm after a relationship."

"Who says I'm not, too?" he asked, their mouths a mere inch apart.

"A monogamous relationship." She chuckled, but the humor didn't penetrate.

The heat of her breath brushed his lips, sending his rapidly beating heart into overdrive. At this moment, he'd vow to never sleep with another woman again if it meant getting between Shay's thighs. And he'd mean it, too.

"I can do monogamy." He'd always been faithful in

relationships. Owning and participating in a sex club didn't mean he was an asshole. His desire to be watched and watch others had nothing to do with plowing the female playing field.

She quirked a brow, her mouth tilting at one side. "I find it hard to believe you'd be faithful with all that muff on display. I noticed the tent in your pants while you were guiding that couple tonight."

"That camping expedition was for you," he murmured against her lips.

She narrowed her gaze. "You didn't even know I was there."

"No. But I knew you weren't far away." He tilted his head, running the tip of his nose along the delicate skin of her cheek. "I wasn't watching Pamela and Jack. I was picturing you and me." He brushed his tongue along the side of her jaw and felt his cock pulse with her barely audible moan. "It was your petite little hands on my body." He nipped the skin below her ear and leaned his pelvis into her, giving his dick the friction it demanded. "It was your sassy mouth all over my cock."

She whimpered and clasped his shoulders. "We shouldn't do this."

"Why?" He had a myriad of reasons, yet none of them penetrated the intoxicating scent he continued to breathe into his lungs. His mouth found the sensitive spot at the base of her neck. He licked. He kissed. He sucked, until she was grinding against his thigh. "You want this. I want this."

She pulled back, blinking away the sexual haze in her eyes. "I want *us*."

She didn't need to add *and nobody else*. The words were already implied. He hung his head, fucking clueless at what to do. He wanted Shay, physically and emotionally, yet ditching one side of his life to obtain her wouldn't work. He'd tried changing himself for others. He'd gone down the vanilla path. Sex in bed with the blinds closed was fine to scratch an itch, but in the long run, he couldn't deny he would eventually want more.

He loved beautiful women, and he loved people watching him fuck beautiful women. It was art, a skill requiring technique and patience. The thrill at having others aroused by the way he touched a woman, making her come apart with his hands, his lips, his cock. Nothing could compare.

Shay was right. They shouldn't be doing this. Because once he laid her beautiful body down, he'd fuck her senseless. Today. Tomorrow. And every other day until the need to drag her to Vault of Sin and make love to her in front of an audience became too much.

"I'll call a cab."

She sucked in a ragged breath, stabbing him through the chest with her anguish. "Okay." Her hands fell from his neck and she slid out from between him and the counter. "Do you mind letting yourself out? I need to have a shower before I collapse."

He nodded, trying to let go of the sinking sensation telling him he was doing the wrong fucking thing. "No problem. I'll see you on Tuesday."

He walked away from her, each footstep harder than dragging his feet through cement. When he reached the door, he paused, his hand on the knob, his back rigid. He wanted to turn around, to give himself one last glance to make sure he was doing the right thing. But leaving was the only option.

One of them had to be willing to change, and from past experience, he knew it couldn't be him. And he sure as hell didn't want to be the one making someone else change their sexual proclivities when he'd fought so hard to be true to his own.

With an exasperated breath, he turned the handle and stepped into the darkness, whispering a silent farewell to the only chance at happiness he'd had in a long time.

# CHAPTER SEVEN

*S*hay rested her hands against the bathroom tiles, letting the hot water rush down her back. She couldn't keep her eyes open, yet when she closed them, all she could see was the dejection in Leo's expression before he strode away from her.

Why was this so hard? It wasn't like she was batting away guys on a nightly basis...well, not decent ones anyway. She should listen to her hormones, enjoy a few hours of hot and dirty sex and then brush it away like any other one-night stand. There was no need for exclusivity.

*Can you say delusional?*

She wrinkled her nose. Her possessive side wasn't going to disappear overnight. If she went to bed with him, she'd want more. Maybe they could play around for a few weeks. With his experience, he could probably teach her a thing or two while getting the fucking out of their systems. Then finally she could move on.

Yeah, right.

She whimpered and raised her face to the water spray. She wanted Leo. Wanted him so much her chest hurt. Surely, if they decided to have fun together and things didn't work out, her loss wouldn't feel any less painful than what she was going through now, would it? It's better to have loved and lost, and all that sappy shit. Right?

"Oh, Christ." She knew this was going to be a mistake, and still she didn't care.

She turned off the water, slammed the shower door open and yanked a towel from the rack. Please don't be gone. She wrapped the plush material around her body, not bothering to dry herself before she secured it above her breasts, and ran from the bathroom.

With her wet hair dripping down her back, she hurried to the front door and flung it open. There was no time to contemplate the inevitable crash and burn as she rushed outside, taking the three steps to her front lawn while searching the darkness. "Leo?"

"Yeah." His voice drifted softly from the porch.

She spun around, finding him in the shadows, seated on her wooden deck chair, hunched over with his elbows on his knees, his head in his hands. He lifted his gaze, the wisps of loose hair framing his face as his soulful eyes stole her breath.

"Oh, good," she squeaked, suddenly feeling like a douche for running into the night in nothing but a towel. "I thought you might have left already."

"I haven't made the call, yet."

"Oh." Awkward. She'd run after him without weighing the consequences and now had no clue what to say.

"What did you want, Shay?"

*You.* She strolled back to the house, this time ascending the three steps leisurely, giving herself a moment to calm down.

"I thought maybe we could give this a try. Take things slow and see where it goes." She shrugged to lessen the impact of her statement and clung to the top of her towel.

"I don't like slow." His voice was smooth as velvet and deep enough to make her nipples tighten. "And you don't want to be with a perverted guy like me."

Her heart clenched. She'd been the cause of his current self-loathing. Her heartless insults from earlier were sinking in, her rejection of his lifestyle, too.

"You're not perverted, Leo. You're just different." She stood at the top of the steps, her bare feet bathed in the warm glow from the lounge room light.

He pushed from his chair, stalking toward her, his face devoid of emotion. "And you want to be different, too?"

She shrugged again. There was nothing blasé about her current emotions, yet she was determined not to show her fear. "I don't know what I want. But I'm willing to test my boundaries a bit."

He gave a derisive chuckle. "A bit?"

She stiffened at his animosity. His bitterness wasn't directed at her, she knew that, yet his scrutiny made her lose confidence.

"Drop the towel."

Oh, boy.

She bit back an anxious retort and raised her chin. He was pushing her away, trying to scare her with his ferocity. Only it had the opposite effect. She wanted to shock him enough to wipe the wicked sneer from his face. To make his eyes widen, his mouth drop. But could she release the towel, exposing herself to anyone who may happen to be awake at this early hour? This was her neighborhood. The place she had to come home to every day.

"See," he taunted, this time taking a step around her and heading for the stairs. "You couldn't handle the shit I'd make you do."

How much do you really want him?

She cursed her nerves and yanked at the towel, releasing

the hold at her breasts. He paused as she let the material fall to the wooden floor, exposing herself to the world.

His nostrils flared, the tight grip on his restraint wavering before her eyes. She jutted her chin, waiting, her chest throbbing harder with each passing second. When the silence continued, she began to realize she wasn't good enough. He wanted a sexual goddess, someone capable of bending to his will in an instant. That change would take time, and with her stubborn streak, probably a lot of patience.

Breaking eye contact, she bent down to scoop up the towel. "Well, I guess there was no harm in trying." She swiveled on her toes and strode to the door. The urge to cover herself was cloying. Instead of succumbing, she remained strong, not giving him the excuse to claim she was scared.

She reached for the handle and paused at the sound of his footfalls pounding behind her. His body slammed against hers, making her gasp as he pushed her against the cold wood.

"Think twice." He gripped her upper arm and yanking her to face him. "Think about what I'll demand of you, and what you're willing to give."

His possession was a scorching balm against her wounded pride. The hardness of his cock pressed between her thighs. The stability of his hands held her tight. "That's all I've done for the past three hours."

He narrowed his gaze, his jaw harsh. "I won't stop this time."

"Well, hurry up and get start—"

He slammed his mouth against hers, pushing his tongue past her lips, searching. He devoured her, kissed her harder than she'd ever been kissed, turning her bones to mush, her strength to weakness. He ran greedy hands down her back, over her bottom and along the underside of her thighs, creating goose bumps in their wake. She gripped his shoulders as he lifted her leg, encouraging her to circle his hip.

"I'll ruin you," he growled into her mouth, thrusting his erection against her pubic bone. His gaze held her captive as her ass began to slam against the wooden door with each of his thrusts.

"You already have." She clawed at his shirt, willing the thin fabric to fall from his shoulders.

She kept her leg in place while he travelled his hand up the underside of her thigh and over her sex. He parted her folds with a finger, sliding it through the slickness of her arousal, and his accompanying throaty groan against her neck had her eyes closing in bliss. He teased her, relentlessly, dragging his finger back and forth, taking her mouth again and again. The slight breeze tickled her skin, an unwanted reminder of the exposure.

"Think of me," he whispered into her mouth. "Only of me."

She nodded. But as Leo's lips moved to her shoulder, her gaze couldn't help travelling to the darkened windows of the house across the street. A group of college kids lived there. They could be watching. Not that they could see much. Leo's bigger frame covered her completely, yet the light from her kitchen filtered through the glass panel beside the door, illuminating them like a flare in the desert.

"My hands, Shay."

She closed her eyes, concentrating on those hands, the way one continued to torment her greedy pussy. The other stroked her side, gently bringing all her nerve endings to life.

"My mouth." He sucked hard on her shoulder, bringing a bite of pain. "My tongue."

She shuddered and reached up to grab the band holding his hair together. She yanked it down and opened her eyes to watch the light-brown strands fall to span along the back of his neck.

"And eventually, my cock."

"Oh, Christ." She couldn't take anymore. She fumbled behind her for the door handle and turned the knob. Together, they stumbled into the house and he slammed the wood shut with the sole of his shoe.

He narrowed his gaze as she stepped back, her chest heaving, her sex throbbing. She could tell what he was thinking, that she couldn't hack being naked outside, and she supposed he was right. To him, being fucked in the open might be a daily ritual. To her, and surely to her neighbors, it wouldn't be so trivial.

"I have condoms in my bedside table," she said as an excuse.

"I have condoms in my pocket." His hair was loose around his cheeks, his dress shirt now untucked and crinkled.

She rolled her eyes, her breaths still coming out in harsh exhalations. "Of course you do."

He let his gaze rake her body. Gradually. Leaving a scorching trail all the way to her toes and up again. "Well, this is your domain now. So, what happens next?"

She sucked her bottom lip between her teeth, her heart a flutter at his raw masculinity.

"Shay, despite my statement earlier, this can go as fast or as slow as you like. There's no preconceptions on my end. If you want to stop, we stop. I just wanted to make sure you knew what you were doing."

"No." She shook her head. "No stopping."

His grin returned as he strode toward her and swept her off her feet. "I was hoping you'd say that."

She squealed—a little in delight, a little in pure adrenaline-filled nervousness. He carried her to the sofa and fell backward onto the cold leather upholstery with her on his lap.

"Straddle me."

She complied, placing her hands on his defined pecs while she spread her legs across either side of his thighs. Her breathing was labored, her heart a rapid pulse behind her ribs.

This was Leo, her boss, the man she'd been fantasizing about for a lifetime. Her dirty dream was finally a reality. Then his hands came to rest on her bare knees and he slowly slid them to her hips and time ceased.

He stared at her with adoration. There was no arrogance, no mildly annoying yet always attractive confidence. His gaze broke her, turning her lust into longing, her fear into anticipation. He was beautiful. His skin so smooth, so perfect. The darkened patch of stubble along his jaw too tempting not to reach out and brush her palm over the rough surface. No man had ever made her insides turn to butter, her brain into a mass of incoherent thoughts.

But nothing happened. He didn't make a move. Didn't speak. Didn't try and alleviate the mindlessness taking over her fluttering heart.

"Leo?"

He frowned. "I don't want to ruin this."

She pulled back at the underlying anger in his voice, unsure who it was directed at. "Umm."

"I don't want to push you or scare you away. Usually, I don't have to worry about what happens after I'm with a woman." His consuming ocean-blue irises made her come undone. "You're different, Shay. I've waited a lifetime for this. Fucking months spent immersed in thoughts of having you hot and ready for me. I've relived those moments in the storeroom over and over and fucking over again. And now that you're here, your pussy hovering over the hardest erection I've had since seventh grade, I'm worried about where to start."

Her cheeks lifted with a smile, one that grew until she was beaming back at him. She ran her hands from his stubble to the loose strands of his hair. "You start by kissing me senseless." She brushed her lips over his and moaned at the way he took possession of her mouth. He scorched her with ferocious licks of his tongue, bringing his hand up to palm the back of her head, to hold her tight.

Her nipples beaded to the point of pain, her sex becoming so hot she was sure she was leaving a wet patch on his trousers. As their tongues tangled, she trailed her hands down, back over his jawline, along his neck to the top button of his shirt. One by one, she undid the buttons and then pulled the shirt wide.

She wanted to look at him, to see the light dusting of hair she could feel beneath her fingers while she stroked his chest. She wanted to mark the skin with her nails, to see his eyes widen or maybe narrow with the pinch of pain. But she couldn't drag her mouth away from his, couldn't stop returning the strokes of tongue and mashing of lips that made her mind blank and her heart all the more attached to this gorgeous man.

"My pants." He spoke into her mouth. "Undo them."

She smiled against his lips. She'd never be a weak woman, easily snapping to comply with a man's demanding order, yet in this moment, with his hands holding her tight and his panted breaths mingling with hers, she could've easily seen herself falling to her knees in submission. Her fingers fumbled with his buckle, releasing the clasp and lowering his zipper.

"Touch me, Shay."

She whimpered, undone by his need. She ran her hand along his crotch, touching the heavy material of his pants and then the softness of silk before stilling on his thick erection. Closing her eyes, she dared not look, trying hard not to grin. The man had a lot to be confident about. He'd brought her undone with his fingers before, but this...this generous length of manliness was going to take her to heaven.

"What are you smirking at?" He tugged her hair until her eyes snapped open.

She giggled, she couldn't help it. The sound was girly and far too feminine, and fuck it, she didn't care. She was high, so damn delirious with lust that she could continue to sound like a virginal school girl and not give a shit.

She wanted the hardened length between her lips, pulsing in her mouth, his hands guiding her to take him deep until he shot down the back of her throat. Without answering, she tilted her head, moving until his hands fell to his sides. Then she backed off his lap, taking herself to the carpeted floor and kneeling between his feet.

His gaze followed her as she gripped the waistband of his pants and boxers, tugged at the material until he raised his ass and helped her lower them down his thighs. His cock stood proud from a patch of dark, trimmed curls, the length jerking toward her. Pre-come beaded his slit, the glistening moisture begging to be tasted. She leaned forward, hovering over him, and blew softly on the flesh she could already taste on her tongue.

"Tease me and I'll return the favor tenfold." He jutted his hips so the head of his shaft bumped her lips.

"That sounds like fun." She poked out her tongue and lightly lapped the salt of his flesh before retreating.

He groaned, the veins in his neck bulging as he threw his head back and gripped the sofa material near his knees. "I'll make sure it isn't." He lifted his head, pinning her with unadulterated lust. "I'll drive you insane. I'll tie you to the bed, bring you to the point of climax for hours on end until you're begging me to fuck you."

Shay pressed her lips together, trying not to smile at what he thought was a threat. If only he knew what she would give to be laid out for his pleasure for hours.

"Don't you like to beg?" She stretched out her tongue to flick the head of his shaft.

He cupped the side of her face, bringing her closer to his length. "This is me begging."

She opened her mouth, emboldened and empowered by the guttural way he growled.

"And when it comes to sex," he grated, "I like everything."

Shay raised a brow, running her tongue down his length and sucking him deep. She built his pleasure, feeling his dick pulse between her lips, ripping a moan from his throat, then she released him with a pop. "Care to elaborate?" She had too many questions when it came to his lifestyle. Only she still wasn't sure if she could handle the answers.

He guided her face back to his cock, encouraging her to take him again. "I've got other things on my mind right now." He smiled down at her, the blue-green of his irises darkening as she took him to the back of her mouth.

She worked the length with her lips and tongue, cupping his sac in her hands, stroking it gently with her fingers. Her sex clenched and the slickness of arousal dampened the inside of her thighs. Pleasure had never been this potent. Sex had never been this exciting. She didn't know if it stemmed from who she was with, how long she'd wanted this, or maybe it was the thrill of arousing a man who seemed to have an insatiable sexual appetite. Either way, her body was burning, craving his touch and aching in the most delicious places.

"Take me all the way in." He moved his other hand to the opposite side of her face. "I want to see those gorgeous lips stretched."

The need to please him was immense. She wanted to make an impact, to stand apart from all the women he'd slept with. Previously, she thought her competition was the unending line of beauties who rubbed up against him on the dance floor of Shot of Sin. Now she knew better. He had eager women at his disposal, ones he didn't have to chat up or flirt with. Women who strolled around in their underwear, who shared the same sexual disposition.

It made her all the more eager to control her breathing and take him as far as she could. Even after relaxing her throat, she still had at least two inches to go. Determination made her push past her gag reflex, taking his full length with eager strokes.

"*Fuck*, Shay." His hips began to buck, pistoning into her mouth, making her lips numb. "Jesus. You're driving me insane...stop."

She didn't listen, needing to make him mindless.

"Shay, *stop*." He grasped her arms, brought her to her feet and yanked her forward to straddle his lap. "Shooting down the back of your throat has been a fantasy of mine. But not tonight." He reached for his pocket and pulled out a condom. "Tonight, I want you riding my cock. I want to see your pretty mouth gasp in pleasure while I make you come."

He could make her orgasm with his dirty words alone. Already, her nipples throbbed and her clit tingled with heightened awareness. She bit her lip as he ripped open the silver packet and rolled the condom down his length. She was starved for him. Impatience clawed at her skin. Need pulsed through her veins. "Hurry the hell up."

Leo chuckled and grabbed the base of his covered shaft. "Ready and waiting, your feistiness."

She could already feel him inside her, could anticipate the delicious stretch of her muscles around him. Her hands were shaking, like a crack addict waiting for a fix. Grabbing his shoulders, she lifted and hovered her pussy above his cock. She closed her eyes, letting the engorged head swipe through her slick juices and across her clit before lowering in one exquisite motion.

Leo moaned as her walls contracted around him, sucking him deeper, holding him tight. He leaned in and rested his head against the side of hers, brushing his lips over the sensitive skin around her ear. "Fucking. Heaven."

She shuddered, taking his compliment to heart. Slowly, she began to undulate, grinding her hips back and forth, leisurely riding him. She set the pace, and Leo followed her lead, kissing her neck in the same soft motion, his hands relaxed and sensual as they explored her body.

Then his lips found hers. He trailed his palms to her breasts and the languid tempo flew out the window. She bucked against him, sucking his tongue into her mouth, delighting in his faint taste of alcohol. He tweaked her nipples and rubbed his calloused palms over the hardened flesh. When his hands grabbed her ass to set his own more punishing rhythm, she let go.

Her pussy clamped tight. Her breathing became erratic as her orgasm began to take over. With one hand, Leo lightly gripped the front of her neck, almost like a choke hold, and lifted her chin so all she could see was him.

She grasped for the top of the sofa behind his shoulders, arching her back while his gaze held her captive. His other hand continued to push her against his cock, the punishing movements making her sight darken in pleasure. She cried out in release, mewling, moaning, screaming to the heavens until the pulsing in her pussy subsided and she had the chance to watch Leo come undone.

His face contorted in lines of strain. He tightened his hand around her throat. "*Fuck*." He roared and the sound reverberated around the room. He smashed his mouth against hers, and gradually, almost imperceptibly, his jolts slowed. The exquisite harshness of his kiss became a languorous mingling of tongues and lips. And when he pulled back, his face was filled with a softness she'd never been on the receiving end of.

"Shay?" His hand fell from her neck.

She quirked a brow and whimpered in reply, her head and eyelids now heavy with exhaustion.

"I think we're both in for a lot of trouble."

# CHAPTER EIGHT

*L*eo pushed from the sofa, his softening dick still inside the sweetest pussy he'd ever plundered. Holy fuck, he was a lost man. Completely disoriented from the brilliance of her sexual appeal.

"Point me toward your room." He yanked up the waist of his pants so they didn't end up around his ankles.

Shay lifted her head from his shoulder and swung a lazy hand toward a darkened hall starting beside the kitchen. "Last door on the right."

She was a deadweight against his chest. Her arms were limp around his shoulders, her legs barely clinging around his waist. He carried her from the room, noticing the lack of frilly, girlie crap through the house. He'd always known her as a guy's girl. Someone more comfortable in a masculine environment, who had a low tolerance for bitchy drama. But tonight, he'd seen her fragile side.

She was still a feminine force to be reckoned with. Only now he'd seen the full picture instead of the layers of bravado she liked to strengthen herself behind. The realization made it harder for him to contemplate things between them not working.

"Fall asleep, baby girl. I'll get you to bed." He was enjoying holding the bundle of vulnerability in his arms. Shay had always been strong, confident, even a little pig-headed. He needed that—someone to keep him on his toes. Yet, he also needed a feminine presence. Someone he could protect. Someone with defenseless moments.

Shay was the brilliant mix of everything he desired. He just needed to figure out a way to remove the petrified look in her eyes every time they discussed Vault of Sin and replace it with something that didn't resemble a brick wall.

"You know I hate when you call me little girl or baby girl, right?" she mumbled against his shoulder. "If you hadn't sucked the life right outta me, I'd smack you."

He smiled, holding back a smart retort. He didn't want to rile her again. The sun would be rising in less than an hour, and she needed rest. And he had to take a clarifying step back. He was falling, way too fast, and at the moment he couldn't find the self-preserving pessimism to make himself stop.

Turning into the last room on the right, he inhaled the heady scent of Shay and held in a moan. The intoxicating mix of vanilla and strawberry would forever remind him of the woman in his arms. The sassy wench who smelled like nirvana. He laid her down, resting her head on a pillow before retreating.

"I'll be back in a sec." He went in search of her bathroom to clean himself up. Minutes later, he was standing at her bedroom door, leaning against the frame, simply watching her.

She lay on her side, her dark silken hair falling over her shoulder. Her breathing was gentle, her lips slightly parted, the faint hint of a contented smile tilting her lips.

"How long are you going to stand there?" she asked, her dark lashes resting against the tops of her smooth cheeks.

*Forever.* "I should go."

Her eyelids fluttered open and she sucked in a lazy breath. "What if I asked you to stay?"

*Ask me, Shay. Grant me one last glimpse of your vulnerability before your mask of strength returns in the morning.* "Is that what you want?"

"Yes." She pulled the sheet up to her chin. "I have questions."

He padded to the other side of her bed, shucked his loosened pants and climbed under the covers. "Ask all you want after you get some sleep."

She shook her head and turned to face him. "No. As tired as I am, I won't rest until we talk."

The dreaded *talk* didn't seem repulsive when discussed from the lips of this gorgeous woman. He slid across to the middle of the bed and rested on one elbow as he faced her. "Then ask."

He'd tell her everything, no matter how ugly the truth may be in her eyes. He'd learned long ago to never lie about his desires. He just needed to get over his own self-loathing.

"Why?" she whispered.

One word had enough meaning to tighten his lungs. He knew what she meant. No clarification necessary. He'd been asked the same thing numerous times, usually in a heated situation, where the word was an accusation, not a question.

"I'm not entirely sure." He shrugged. "It's an addiction of sorts."

Shit. Shay winced at his confession and he rushed to clarify. "Not to sex." He stroked a hand down her cheek. "I think I'm hooked on the rush of pride that follows a woman's orgasm at my hands. I love bringing pleasure. Making someone fall apart is a powerful thing. And having others watch only heightens the sensation."

She paid no attention to the stroke of his hand. She was emotionally detaching herself, taking a step back even in her almost comatose state. "So Vault of Sin is a part of your life you can't live without?"

He sucked in a silent breath, not wanting to push her away and not able to lie either. "A woman has the ability to change a man." He ran his finger under her chin, sliding his thumb along her lower lip.

"I don't want to change you." She frowned, clutching the sheet tighter to her chest.

"I know. And I appreciate that." He wanted so badly to sink his finger between her lips, to feel the rough surface of her tongue against his skin. To change the serious situation to something pleasurable. "I'm prepared to try, Shay. I think that's all that matters at the moment."

"Mmm." Her lids drifted shut. "I want to make you happy," she murmured. "I'm just not sure I can be the woman you need."

He remained quiet, listening to her breathing as it became heavier. Even in sleep she was alluring. He lay beside her, continuing to stroke her hair, pulling the sheet down a little to admire the flawless skin of her neck and shoulder. Things between them wouldn't be easy. Their hurdles were large and overbearing. But taking the chance would be worth it. He could risk rejection one last time. For her.

He just needed to make sure T.J. and Brute were onboard.

The club was a part of the three of them, something Shay probably hadn't realized, yet. They all spent time downstairs. They all watched. Leo only hoped he was nearby when she figured out being a part of his lifestyle also meant being a part of Brute and T.J.'s too.

# CHAPTER NINE

Shay woke up on her stomach with a tickling sensation at the low of her back. She frowned, her eyes still closed, and wriggled in an attempt to make it stop.

"It's already past lunch time, gorgeous."

She moaned, tilting her head to the deep, smooth voice, and opened one eye a crack. Beside her was the rough-stubbled face of the sexiest man alive.

"Go away," she groaned and slammed the pillow over her head. Sexy as sin or not, nobody got away with waking her. It was bad enough on a night she'd slept soundly, but last night, or the early hours of today, it had been a constant struggle to stop her mind from churning.

"You sure you don't want to wake up?"

He smoothed his hand over her ass, delving between her crack to the heat of her pussy. He stroked her to life with two greedy fingers, making her wet within moments, tearing needy whimpers from her throat.

"Leo."

"Yeah." He pulled the sheet off her in a flourish and then

the heavy weight of his body moved over hers. "You still want to go back to sleep?"

He ground his erection into her ass, the tip of his rubber-covered shaft teasing her until she had to bite the sheets to stop herself from moaning. His hips undulated, his cock inching lower, sinking to the place her body craved him to be. Then he was at her entrance, rubbing himself along her slit, sliding through her arousal.

"Your body may be asleep, but your pussy definitely isn't," he drawled with a chuckle.

She threw her pillow away and bucked, trying to get his self-righteous ass off her. "Don't be a jerk."

His weight became heavier against her back, the almost silent sound of his breathing brushing her ear. "Tell me to stop and I will. But I'll never apologize for craving your body."

Her heart fluttered as he stilled.

"Want me to get off, Shay?"

Her name on his lips was the most alluring sound she'd ever heard. It brought a smile to her mouth and a tingling throb to her muscles. "No." She tilted her ass so his cock head penetrated. Never.

He surged forward in a deep thrust, stealing her breath and replacing it with ecstasy. Her body welcomed him, squeezing around his length as he began to leisurely thrust.

"I've been watching you for hours," he murmured into her neck, blazing a trail of kisses along her shoulder.

She moaned, enjoying the delicious friction of skin against skin. His mouth hot and biting, his undulations smooth and languorous. "I was dreaming about you."

"Hmm? What was I doing?"

Shay closed her eyes, playing back the scene in her mind. They'd been at the club. Downstairs. In the darkened corner of one of the rooms. She was seated between Leo's thighs, her back to his chest, her hands on the hard muscle above his knees, while his fingers worked their way into her jeans and under the waistband of her panties.

They were watching a couple on the bed in the center of the room. The man was buff, blond, his face shadowed in the darkness while he fed his cock into an eager woman's mouth. Their movements were like a dance, melodic, hypnotizing and dream-time-Shay couldn't contain the slick arousal saturating Leo's fingers.

Now she wondered if watching another couple would be equally enjoyable in real life. Were her boundaries that easy to break?

"We were at work."

"In the storeroom? Being with you in there has haunted me for months. It killed me to walk away."

And to continue walking. She wanted to add. He'd never come back, not emotionally, not until last night anyway.

"No. We were at Vault of Sin. Watching."

She squeezed her muscles around his shaft and his answering groan sent a shiver down her spine.

"Please tell me you liked it."

Shay stopped, taking a moment to let the seriousness of his plea sink in. The club was a part of him. A place he would feel incomplete without. Even if he was willing to step away, even temporarily, it wouldn't change the fact he still yearned to go there.

Slowly, she nodded. "Yes. It was hot as hell."

He climbed off her, grabbed her hip and flipped her onto her back. She stared wide-eyed as he moved over her again, this time resting against her belly, his gaze narrowing on hers while his cock found its home. He entered her with care, gradually penetrating, letting every inch of him fill her while he watched the pleasure take hold. "What does that mean?"

Her focus waivered as he lowered his lips to her nipple

and sucked the hardening peak into his mouth. Tingles ricocheted through her body, and she circled his hips with her thighs, needing more.

"I don't know," she murmured. "I think my subconscious is willing to see what happens."

He raised a brow, acknowledging the enormity of her statement. Instead of voicing the happiness she could see curving his lips, he merely moved to the other nipple to pay homage.

"I guess my subconscious is a dirty little whore," she added, slightly flustered by the ferocity in his eyes.

He chuckled and his puffed breaths brushed the sensitive skin of her breast. "Enjoying sex doesn't make you a whore." He thrust inside her, drawing a cry from her throat. "Watching others play doesn't make you dirty." His hips plunged harder. "I promise you, Shay, you'll never be left wanting if you're with me."

This time, his cock made her scream in delight.

Leo leaned in, stroking her lips apart with his tongue. "Just give me a chance."

She nodded, undone by his sincerity, captured by his raw plea. "I'll try," she whispered, raising her hips to meet his next slide home.

He burned her with his kiss, smashing his mouth against her with the same ferocity as his hips pounded. He drove her wild, he made her crazy, and all the while she could feel herself slipping more in love with him. With matched aggression, she clenched her thighs around him and dug her nails into the skin of his back.

"Wait." She broke their kiss, not wanting to come yet. Her pussy was already pulsing in anticipation, her limbs taut. She extended her neck, gasping for air. But he didn't quit, didn't stop thrusting into her, driving her pleasure higher. "I said stop. I don't want to come yet."

"You've got no say in the matter." He scraped his teeth up her neck. "I want to feel your pussy milking me. I want to see those pretty brown eyes roll back as you come undone."

"Leo," she warned, nudging closer and closer to the precipice with each undulation. Next Saturday was likely to break them, so she had to make now last forever.

"Fall apart for me, Shay."

His whisper against her ear was too much. She complied, her breathing coming in hard gasps as she tightened around his cock and rode the wave of orgasm. She drowned in the bliss, her hips continually reaching up to meet his thrusts until Leo swore and followed after her.

His lips continued to love her, his hands adoring with their gentle glide across her skin. As his movements came to a halt, her eyelids became droopy and she groaned with the need for sleep.

"You do wonders for a guy's self-esteem," he chuckled, sliding from her body.

"I try my best." She stretched, loving the delicious aches his lovemaking had left in her muscles.

The mattress dipped as he stood and strode for the bathroom, returning moments later with the smile she adored.

"Can I make you breakfast?" He waggled a brow. "Naked?"

She laughed, overcome by the dreamy warmth overtaking her chest. For too long, she'd been one of those women who'd believed men weren't a necessity in a strong woman's life. She was relatively successful. She paid her own bills. And her body would never be left unsatisfied with the big box of toys under her bed. But something about the way he looked at her made her feel empowered. His smile increased her confidence. His touch made her invincible. "I only have cereal."

"If you don't mind me driving your car, I can go pick something up."

"Naked?"

His smile widened. "Unfortunately, I don't think that's an option."

"Ahh, so you do have limits."

His humor gently faded. "I have many limits, Shay."

The quick slide into thoughts of Vault of Sin made the warmth inside her vanish. "Cereal it is." She climbed from the bed, and strode her naked ass to the walk-in closet, returning seconds later with a thin silk dressing gown.

"That's not going to happen." Leo eyed her clothing and crossed his arms over his chest. "Take it off."

Annoyance, or was that anticipation, shot up her spine. She raised a brow, coming to stand in front of him. "Is this where any normal woman would whimper and obey?"

His lip curled, predatory and too damn sexy for her to ignore. "This is where you take that off or I'll do it for you."

Her nipples hardened, already yearning for more of his touch. She grinned, shrugged and then made a move to walk around him, because that's what stubborn women do.

In a flash, she was spun back around. In seconds, rough hands stripped her naked. Then, in a few erratic beats of her heart, the sash was yanked from her dressing gown and Leo grabbed her, tying her hands behind her back.

She stood, shocked and silent in her hallway, wondering what the hell had just happened.

"Thank you," he taunted. "I actually enjoy doing things the hard way."

By the look of his growing erection, he wasn't lying. "Point taken. You can untie me now." She tried to purr, to be the seductive princess who would woo him with her charm, but he didn't succumb. Instead, he grinned the sly, arrogant grin that annoyed her and made her melt all at once.

"Nice try." He strode forward, grabbed the tie at her joined wrists and guided her forward. "It's time for breakfast."

# CHAPTER TEN

*L*eo raised the toast to Shay's mouth, enjoying the way her naked chest delicately rose and fell as she ate. He should be thankful she denied him the choice to spoon-feed her cereal. The exercise would've ended in him *accidentally* pouring milk down her cleavage, watching the trail fall between those gorgeous breasts before finally licking it off when it came close to reaching the heat of her pussy.

He needed to keep his hands off her. To make her understand this thing between them wasn't based on sex. And to also give her time to think. He admired her strength and confidence above all else. So seeing her skittish at the mere mention of the Vault was something he needed to focus on resolving.

"Juice?" He placed the half-eaten piece of jam covered toast back on the plate in front of her.

She nodded. "Thank you."

He settled the glass against her lips, taking care to tip it at the right pace. He enjoyed caring for her, being the one making sure her needs were met. If he had more restraint, he'd stick around all day, keeping her hands tied as he catered to her every need. But it was only a matter of time before his dick took control.

"More toast?" He lowered the glass to the table and fought the need to kiss the juice from her mouth.

"No. I'm good." She nibbled her bottom lip. "But you can untie me."

"Soon." He cleaned away their cups and plates and stacked them in the dishwasher as Shay watched from the stool behind the kitchen counter. "I like having you defenseless for once."

She scoffed. "I'm always defenseless around you."

He copied her, scoffing louder. "The only time you've shown any vulnerability..." apart from what he'd witnessed in the last twelve hours, "...was the first night you worked the bar in Taste of Sin." Or maybe the days after he'd pleasured her in the storeroom.

She cringed, the tops of her cheeks turning the slightest shade of pink. "You remember that?"

He'd remembered every moment since she'd handed in her employment application. "I recall with vivid clarity, T.J. remarking on how cute you were at the start of your shift. He thought you were sweet and innocent." He closed the dishwasher and brushed the crumbs off his palms into her sink. "It didn't take long for him to determine those deep brown eyes were hiding a little minx."

She hit him with a dazzling smile. "Once the doors closed for the night, the three of you took pleasure in testing me. You barked off drink orders, making sure I knew how to prepare everything from memory."

He inclined his head. He'd never laughed harder in his life. One by one, Leo, Brute and T.J. had thrown names of cocktails at her, until finally T.J. requested a Crouching Tiger shot and they'd all been too drunk to notice she'd placed a mix of Sambuca, Tequila and Tabasco sauce in front of them instead.

"T.J. hadn't known what hit him."

"For a second, I thought he was going to die, he was choking so hard." She started to laugh, making those tempting breasts bounce. "I was glad you guys didn't fire me."

He ignored the way his cock jerked and made his way back to her side. It was time to leave. He wanted this moment to stick with him until Tuesday—her beautiful smile, the lush curve of her breasts, the way her hair fell like silk against her smooth skin.

"That was never an option." He untied the material at her wrists and helped her to her feet. "You fit in perfectly."

A little too perfectly at times. The three of them held a soft spot for Shay. She may have a temper, but her few bad days had never come close to outweighing the good. She always made them smile, either with her over-exaggerated annoyances or with her sassy, flirting banter.

"I'm glad you think so." She fell into him, resting her arms on his chest as she stared up at him.

He was falling—into desire, under her spell. "It's time for me to go."

Her brow furrowed the slightest bit and she stepped back. "You don't want to stay?"

"If I thought it was the right thing to do, I wouldn't leave until we had to go back to work on Tuesday." He grabbed her hand, entwined their fingers and tried to ease the dejection in her eyes. "But I bailed out on Travis last night. I need to call him and make sure Vault of Sin was closed without drama."

∼

*V*ault of Sin—three innocent words potent enough to make Shay's stomach flutter. She nodded, trying not to let the passing seconds daunt her. She'd been in the zone, tied up like a little love slave waiting to be satisfied. And now he was leaving.

*Look out toys, here I come.*

"Are you sure you're comfortable working down there next Saturday?" Concern tainted his voice. "There's no pressure if you don't. I'll work the bar myself if I have to."

And be surrounded by voluptuous women vowing for his attention? "No. I can do it."

In the future, working her usual shift at Shot of Sin would be painful, knowing what Leo would be experiencing downstairs. Her imagination would be the death of her. She needed to face her fears head on, while also keeping him in her sights.

"You'll see me in the restaurant during the week and my shift at the club bar on Friday, so there's plenty of time to grill me beforehand. On Saturday, I can arrive early to check things out properly. You know, without all that cock staring me in the face."

It was meant as a joke, but Leo stiffened. "If you're uncomfortable—"

"I'm fine." She groaned. "Please, stop asking."

He leaned into her, moving to eye level. "Shay..."

"Don't." She pushed at his muscled chest and glanced away. She was intimidated, jealous, and yeah, maybe at the top of the nervous scale, but it didn't mean she was a chicken shit. "I said I'd try. This is me trying. I don't need you treating me like a little girl."

"Okay," his voice softened. "But if you change your mind all you have to do is tell me."

She nodded. "I need to get dressed."

They both knew it was a dismissal of the conversation. She didn't care. She was sick of worrying about it. Sick of thinking about it. Turning on her heel, she hastened down the hall in search of her dressing gown.

"I'll also need to show you the back entrance to the club, so make sure you remind me on Friday." Leo strode behind her, following her into her bedroom.

"Back entrance?" She peered over her shoulder, immediately engrossed by the flexing muscles of his arms as he reached for his clothes on the floor.

He glanced up from beneath thick, dark lashes and grinned. "I think I told you it was the delivery entrance when you first started."

Lying little bastard. "Anything else you've lied about?" She raised a brow and the humor died from his features.

"I've only ever lied to keep the club safe. Legally, it shouldn't be running within the walls of Shot of Sin." He pulled on his shirt, doing up the buttons as his gaze scrutinized her. "If we asked for government approval for a sex club, the local public would be notified. The anonymity of members would be breached, and I'm sure you could imagine the shit fight we'd have on our hands from do-gooders and religious groups." He straightened his collar and then yanked on his pants. "But now you know there's no need for secrecy between us. I won't lie to you. Even if the truth is brutal, I'll take a leaf out of Brute's book and let you have it straight." He stalked toward her and came to a stop at her feet.

Leo stroked a hand through her sleep-tangled hair. "I stayed away from you for a long time, wanting to ensure I didn't hurt you. So, whatever it takes, please know I have your best interest at heart."

Shay inhaled deeply and let it out on a sigh.

Okay, so maybe she was a little fragile. The thought of rejection sat like a lead balloon beneath her ribs. She was a grown woman, confident in every aspect of her life...up until this moment. Now she had to question if she was adventurous enough for Vault of Sin.

Only time would tell. All she knew was that being intimate with Leo and then going back to a platonic relationship wasn't an option her heart could handle. She was risking a lot with the hasty decisions she'd made during the early hours of the morning. And now it was too late to go back.

He leaned in, tilting her chin, bringing them a breath apart. "The only truth I have for you right now is that I want you. Any way I can." His eyes searched hers, focusing with heated intent so potent her body flushed. "Let's see where it takes us."

Shay bit her lip, fighting the need to wrap her hands around his neck and drag him back onto the bed. "I'll see you Tuesday then."

"Yeah. You will." He brushed his mouth over hers and then stepped back. "Just try and keep your wanton hands off me in front of the other staff, okay?" He grinned and headed for the door.

"You're an arrogant jerk," she called, her gaze trained on his sexy ass as he strutted from the room.

"A jerk you're now stuck with."

His steps retreated, each soft footfall making her want to yell for him to come back. She was hooked. Not just to his charm or the way he worked her body, but to the thought of them being together. The image of them holding hands had her turning all girlie with the yearning to squee.

Now all they had to do was get over their myriad of issues.

# CHAPTER ELEVEN

*T*uesday morning took forever to arrive. Leo stood behind the Taste of Sin bar, waiting for the lunch staff to show up for work. One in particular. He'd spent the last two days distracting himself from calling, texting, emailing or even sending flowers to Shay.

The harder he tried to occupy his mind, the more potent his memories of her delicious body became. He'd thrashed himself at the gym, replied to a full inbox of work-related crap and even cleaned out his fridge. All before Sunday night arrived.

Now he couldn't wait for the next thirty minutes to tick by until she showed up for her shift. He wasn't just pussy-whipped, he was wrangled, tangled and tied to the bed waiting to be decimated.

He felt like a kid at an amusement park, all giddy excitement and nervous anticipation. Reality hadn't left the building. He still knew they had a shitload of problems to discuss and resolve, but finding a woman like Shay and having her stick around after learning his sordid secrets was an opportunity worthy of a little crazy optimism.

The first hurdle had been the hardest, and they'd sailed over the fucker with the grace of an Olympic champion. Okay, maybe his hindsight was skimming the Saturday night drama. He couldn't help it. His enthusiasm was out of control.

They both needed time. Flipping from a work relationship to lovers wasn't easy in a normal business environment. When a sex club was brought into the mix, it was like walking through a minefield. But instead of explosives, they were contending with jealousy, spite, judgments and lies.

He needed to make sure they avoided each detonation.

Every other woman had balked at his lifestyle choices. And he understood why. It wasn't common to share the person you cared for, and stripping in the middle of a crowded room wasn't on everyone's bucket list. Yet, Shay was still sticking around. She'd made him crazy with her curves, driven his desire to insatiable heights, and now he couldn't quit thinking about ways to make this work.

The front door swooshed open, stealing his attention, and there she was, in tight black pants, a white-collared shirt and the glow of the sun surrounding her in a halo.

"Morning." His gaze was glued to her, drinking her in as if he hadn't seen her in years.

"Morning." She grinned. "How were your days off?"

*Unending.* "Fine. You?" He strode around the bar and met her in the middle of the room filled with tables and chairs.

"Fine."

He stepped into her, wove his arm around her waist and tugged her softness against him. She'd arrived early and no other bar staff or waitresses were here. Apart from the chefs hidden in the kitchen out the back, they were alone. It gave him the perfect opportunity to take the edge off his craving.

"I missed you." His mouth found hers, kissing, nipping, licking until they both had to come up for air.

"I thought I was meant to keep my hands off you."

"You were." He pecked her lips. "You're not doing a very good job."

Her eyes twinkled, desire and sass staring back at him. "For such an accomplished man, you have very little restraint."

"And for such a flirty woman, you're doing a great job of brushing me off."

"I'm not brushing you off." She had the gall to gape at him with mock outrage. "It's just that my boss is a hard-ass and I don't want to get in trouble."

"Sometimes getting in trouble is the best part."

He'd never get enough of her quick-witted charm. Even the subtle changes in her expression added to her potent mix of confidence and sexuality. She knew how to work him. Hell, she probably knew how to work every man. But he didn't care. Shay was his now.

"True." She pressed her lips together, the corners of her mouth tilting in barely contained laughter.

He leaned in for another kiss, already tasting her on his tongue when she tilted her head away.

"Not here," she whispered, practically castrating him with the rejection.

She'd broken him, made him weak and lust-crazed in the one place he demanded control. All he wanted to do is strip her bare and sink into her over and over. Right now, he didn't care if the timid restaurant staff caught them. He didn't give a shit if his club secrets were exposed. His desire for her had already tightened his balls, making his shaft thicken with anticipation. His brain was deprived of blood flow and all the fucks he should've given about being caught were nowhere to be found. "Did you even think about me?"

"Of course." She smiled up at him, this time with genuine admiration. "I couldn't stop."

"And what about the Vault?" Regret hit him the same moment she stiffened in his arms. He should've stopped before curiosity got the better of him. Now the playfulness had left her features, replaced with discomfort.

"The jury's still out on that one."

"There's no rush. I can wait." He wasn't going to push or pry. He shouldn't have opened his mouth in the first place. Patience was the only option if this was going to work. He just needed to pull his dick into line.

She pushed gently at his chest, disentangling herself from his arms. "I need to get ready, otherwise my arrogant boss might fire my ass."

He groaned, long and low. Today would be torture, tomorrow too, and every other fucking day until he could get his fill of this beautiful woman. "Meet me in the storeroom in ten minutes." He was joking. At least he thought he was.

Shay's chuckle filled the room and she shook her head as the front door opened again. "I don't think those duties are in my job description."

He wanted to chase her, to stalk her into the nearest corner and show her exactly what duties he required of her. Only problem was they couldn't be caught together. He needed to explain the situation to T.J. and Brute first, and the two of them wouldn't turn up until later.

Staff and management relationships weren't forbidden. They'd worked together long enough to trust one another to make the right judgments, but when Vault of Sin was involved, they all second-guessed every decision they made. Because of the privacy issues and the lurid nature of what happened downstairs, they had to tread carefully. Shay was a liability now she knew their secret, and none of them liked any type of vulnerability when it came to their private club.

"We'll discuss this later," he called, and then growled when she replied with a girlie finger wave over her shoulder.

The lunch rush came and went, with Shay acting oblivious to his constant stare. He was sure she was deliberately teasing him. Torturing him. Making him so fucking crazy he ended up approaching her while serving a customer and asked her to meet him in the storeroom for a private discussion.

"I'll be there in a minute."

He stalked away and closed the storeroom door behind him to wait in peace. Time ticked by, hours, minutes... probably seconds, he couldn't tell the difference anymore. Then she opened the door and closed it quietly behind her before launching herself at him.

He stumbled back, hitting the stacked shelves, making the rows of bottles clang. They paused, making eye contact as the noise lessened, waiting for the all-clear to go ahead. Then Shay's gaze snapped to the shelf behind him and she frantically reached her arm out before a loud smash filled the room.

"Shit." She slid away from him.

As the heat of her fled his body, his heart rate quickened. He didn't give a fuck about the bottle, or the mess, or whatever the cost of the alcohol. His mind was only focused on one thing.

"I'll clean it up later." He grabbed her arms and pulled her back against his chest.

Passion flared in her eyes and she clung to him as he lowered his hands to the delicious curve of her ass. He kissed her, hard, while she relaxed into the grip of his hold and began wrapping her legs around his waist, climbing him, her hands everywhere. He smiled against her mouth, loving every breath of sweet-scented perfume, every soft whimper, every clench of her thighs around him.

"You're killing me," she rasped. "How am I meant to work with you watching my every move? I can't concentrate."

He yanked at her waistband, unbuckled the belt, flicked open the button. "You looked fine to me."

She clawed his shirt, sliding her hands under the material to run her fingernails against his skin. "I had to re-do three orders."

"I had to leave the service area to readjust my cock fifteen times."

She chuckled into his mouth, charming his tongue with hers, while her fingers glided through his hair. "I love knowing you're—"

The click of the door handle made him freeze and Shay stiffened against him. He didn't have time to move before the door flung open and a faint gasp had him closing his eyes with a wince.

*Fuck.* He glanced over his shoulder, finding the pale complexion of one of their female chefs. Her eyes were wide, her mouth agape. She shook her head, blinking away the shock and stepped back into the hall.

"Ahh..." Her gaze travelled between him and Shay, the high of her cheeks darkening. "I didn't mean to... I'm...ahh... sorry." She slammed the door shut, leaving them in silence to listen to the quickening pace of her shoes thumping down the hall.

*Damn it.*

Leo remained still, letting his idiocy sink in as he held Shay against him. He was the boss. He couldn't be pulling this crap at work. At least not upstairs where fucking in public wasn't expected.

"I'm sorry." Shay climbed off him and straightened her shirt.

"Not your fault." He righted his clothes and helped smooth out her tangled hair. He had no clue what he looked

107

like, but Shay's blouse was crumpled and her hair well and truly mussed. She practically had *storeroom-fucker* tattooed on her forehead. If only they'd crossed the finish line to make it worthwhile.

"Do I look okay?" She glanced up at him, her pupils wide with concern.

"Umm."

She winced. "I look ridiculous, don't I?"

"You look like a woman who was caught rutting in the storeroom."

"Great." With one hand, she combed her fingers through her hair while the other pulled a hair tie from her pocket.

No, not great. He hadn't found the right moment to speak to T.J. and Brute yet, and he needed to get to them before the gossip mill.

"Shay, I'm sorry, but I've gotta speak to the guys before they find out what's going on from someone else." He kissed her temple and gripped her shoulders. "Will you be okay?"

She pulled a face, half funny, half awkward. "Yeah. Go."

"I'll meet you at your car when you finish your shift." Outside. Alone. Where they wouldn't be caught acting like secretive teenagers.

She nodded. "I'll clean up the mess."

He eyed the pool of alcohol and glass on the floor at the end of the shelves. "Damn it." He'd forgotten about the broken bottle. "I'll make it up to you. Promise." He gave her one last kiss and then stalked to the door, turned the handle and yanked it open to find Brute staring back at him. His friend was leaning against the wall, arms crossed over his chest, a fucked-off expression etched across his face.

Could this moment get worse?

"We need to talk," Brute growled.

Yes, apparently, it could.

# CHAPTER TWELVE

*L*eo gave Brute ten minutes to cool his temper before he strode into the empty Shot of Sin night club.

"Speak of the devil."

He lifted his gaze as he approached the main bar and found T.J. swiveling around on his bar stool.

"About time." Brute turned from stocking chip packets behind the counter.

Leo ignored the jab and took a seat beside T.J. The three of them needed to talk, only the look on Brute's face said there wouldn't be a lot of civility involved.

"T.J. just finished filling me in on the stalker drama of Saturday night." Brute leaned against the counter on the other side of the bar, his gaze scrutinizing. "Please tell me you didn't sleep with her."

Leo winced.

"Fucking hell, man. Are you kidding me?" Brute's voice rose with each word, sparking Leo's anger.

"My free time is none of your business." It was a lie, a vain attempt to gain some ground over Brute's holier-than-thou attitude. Leo knew he was in the wrong. He should've told them about Shay as soon as they arrived. Better yet, he should've called them Sunday morning. But sometimes Brute's asshole attitude robbed him of his ability to think clearly, and all he could do was come back swinging.

"It is when you're shoveling your dick into one of our employees during business hours."

True, yet Leo didn't need a lecture. And Brute rarely listened to reason. For once, Leo wanted to be happy. To hold a tiny piece of merriment in his long-frozen chest and hope for the best. He slid from the stool and stepped back, ready to cut and run.

"Wait." T.J. grabbed Leo's upper arm. "You both need to calm down so we can discuss this."

Leo jerked off the hold and returned Brute's glare. "Then talk instead of being a fuckin' jerk."

A pregnant pause followed, nothing but the clang of pans echoing into the empty room from their adjoining restaurant.

"You know this can't end well," Brute finally muttered.

"Fucking this up isn't inevitable." It was highly likely, just not inevitable. "We're both taking it slow. Shay is willing to learn more about the lifestyle, so we're going to see where this takes us."

"Banging her in the storeroom is slow?" Brute shook his head and scoffed "And besides, Shay's been drooling over your ass for months. I'm pretty sure she'd do anything for a bone."

"Watch yourself." Leo pointed a furious finger across the bar. "I know the risks. I've been through this before."

"And obviously you didn't learn a thing. Does she realize what your lifestyle involves? Have you thoroughly discussed it? Because a few hours working in the Vault doesn't even scratch the surface of what goes on down there."

*Fuck you.*

Leo ground his teeth and turned his back to stare across the vacant dance floor. This was not what he expected from his friends. Yes, they'd all endured the same bullshit and broken relationships due to the club, but it didn't mean they had to ditch the idea of ever having a stable partner. Shay was his one chance to turn things around.

"Leo, it's not our business to dictate what you do. Or who you do," T.J. started. "But you're putting us all at risk. I didn't realize how much until Brute pointed it out."

"Of course he pointed it out." Leo swung back to face them. "Making others miserable is his M.O."

"That's not what this is about." The anger in Brute's gaze softened and he let out a huff. "We have a lot to lose."

"I'm aware."

Shay would no longer be able to work for them if this thing between them blew up in their faces. She'd have to walk, leaving them short staffed and Leo nursing another busted ego.

"Really?" Brute asked. "So you've thought about how much of a bull-headed spitfire she is? You fuck her over and she's going to fight back first and ask questions later."

Leo froze, swallowing over the ache tightening his throat. Shay was quick to lash out in armament, but she was professional...most of the time. "She wouldn't do anything stupid."

"And you're willing to put Vault of Sin on the line with that assumption?" Brute gave a derisive laugh. "For a smart guy, you're acting pretty fucking dumb."

"You two were the ones who forced this. Not me." His chest pounded with fury. None of this would've happened if they hadn't encouraged her to work downstairs. "I didn't want her down there in the first place."

"She was meant to work the bar, not your cock," Brute bit back.

"Calm down." T.J.'s demand reverberated off the walls. "For fuck's sake, take a breath, both of you."

Leo's nostrils flared as he tried to settle his rampant breathing. It wasn't only fury at Brute being an unsympathetic bastard making him hyperventilate. It was the fact his business partner was right about Shay's temperament. She was stubborn, and her initial reaction when hurt was to bite back. If Leo ran the business by himself and the risk of backlash only fell on his shoulders, maybe it wouldn't be so bad. But moving forward was dangerous to T.J., Brute, Vault of Sin and all the patrons who felt at home within its walls.

*Fuck.*

His mind had rested solely on the outcome of losing Shay as a friend and bartender. God knew his experience with backstabbing women was first-class. He should've contemplated every direction this relationship could turn instead of letting himself concentrate on the carnality.

"I'll print out a non-disclosure statement," T.J. broke the silence. "Exactly the same as the one we made Travis and Tracy sign. Then Shay will know the legal ramifications of exposing the Vault."

"Go ahead." Brute grunted. "But we all know it won't do shit when the club is running illegally."

Leo tried not to crumple under the weight of guilt pressing down on his chest and ran a weary hand over his face. Lack of sleep wasn't helping his ability to figure this shit out. He'd been too overcome by lust and the hope he'd finally found someone to accept his desires to be able to get more than a few hours' sleep over the last two nights.

This had to work. Somehow. He needed Shay, but he also needed the club and his friends by his side. "What should I do?" He grimaced when his voice waivered.

Brute sucked in a heavy breath. "Stay away from her."

"No." Leo shook his head, not in anger, not in defiance, but in resignation. He couldn't stay away. Today had proven he wasn't strong enough.

"I don't mean forever. Just a week or two. Let her think things over and make up her own mind without your sleazy pheromones playing havoc with her judgment. If she turns up to her shift at Vault of Sin this Saturday, at least we'll know she's taken the first step by herself."

"It'll also give us time to see if she can separate work and play," T.J. added. "Having you in the office doing the books isn't uncommon. Keep your distance. At least for a little while."

Leo gave a defeated laugh. "And you think Shay's going to be okay with being ignored? She'll be pissed." She'd be fucking furious.

"If this is about commitment and not just sex, she'll wait."

T.J. nodded. "I'm sorry, but I think it's necessary. I know I joked about you being with her, but we all risked a lot to open Vault of Sin. I'd feel better if I knew how serious she was taking this."

"We'll keep an eye on her for you." Brute lowered his voice, the hostility finally leaving his tone. "Unfortunately, with the way things have gone in the past, I think we need to be extra careful. None of us want to see another crash and burn."

"Yeah. I get it." Leo rubbed the tension from the back of his neck and let his last ounce of excitement fade away.

He owed T.J. and Brute peace of mind. Hell, if one of them were shacking up with a staff member, Leo would probably feel the same apprehension. Each of them had a cross to bear in relation to their desires. Brute had been open and honest about his sexual activities, not holding back with his friends and family when they found out. He'd taken their disapproval in his stride, closing himself off to each and every one of them, becoming more heartless with every lost tie and no longer giving a shit about who he offended.

While T.J. had done the opposite and run before he could

inflict pain on himself or others. He'd left a beautiful wife and a promising future because he couldn't stand to taint the woman he loved. And neither Leo nor Brute blamed him. People had strong beliefs when it came to sex. Many of which couldn't be swayed. Only he couldn't walk away from Shay with no explanation and expect her to be waiting for him at the end of the week.

"I need to warn her first." He already dreaded the conversation. "I'll catch her in the parking lot before she leaves tonight."

"Do what you need to do."

"Just be mindful of all the players involved," Brute added.

Right. Leo turned on his heel and made his way back toward the Shot of Sin entrance.

"It'll work out for the best," T.J. called.

Leo scoffed. Women never wanted to be pushed away, and he'd already seen firsthand how Shay reacted to rejection. Too bad for him, he'd used all his luck on her over the weekend. What he needed now was a miracle.

# CHAPTER THIRTEEN

*S*hay sauntered across the parking lot, smothering her elated grin at the sight of Leo leaning against the side of her car. The sun was fading, the birds chirping, and there he stood, a sight to behold in his suit pants and business shirt.

*Wakey, wakey, uncontrollable hormones.*

She'd been worried earlier, not knowing how Brute and T.J. would react to the storeroom issue or their relationship in general. But Leo hadn't come back to speak to her, so she assumed everything had worked out for the best. Good thing too, because she didn't know how they were going to hide this connection between them when they couldn't even keep their hands off each other.

"I hope you weren't waiting long."

The idea of him waiting at all made her belly flutter. Never before had she been a giddy girlfriend...or lover...or whatever the hell this was. The mere sight of Leo had her body on high alert.

"No."

She ignored his gruff tone and sidled up to him, yanking

her handbag strap onto her shoulder. They'd only spent one night together, yet he'd instilled enough confidence in their future for her to wrap her hands around his neck and press her body into his. "Do you want to come back to my place tonight?"

Her stomach dropped when he stiffened, his lips thinning to a tight line. He looked straight through her. There was no heat or passion in his expression. Nothing. Only cold disengagement.

"Leo?" When he remained silent, she dropped her hands and stepped back. "What's going on?"

"Sorry." He blinked the light back into his eyes and reached for her. "Nothing's wrong. I just need to discuss a few things with you."

She brushed away his touch and remained out of reach. "That sounds delightfully ominous."

"It isn't." His words lacked the enthusiasm to back up the statement.

"Well, spill." She crossed her hands over her chest and it didn't skip her attention that he ignored the intentional plumping of her breasts. Something was wrong. Big time.

"I'm going to be in the office all week, so we probably won't get a chance to see each other."

She frowned, fixing him with a what-the-fuck expression. "That's it?"

He shrugged. "Yeah. I told you it was nothing." The indifference in his voice said otherwise. "I doubt if I'll get the chance to see you until Saturday night. I need to plow through a heap of book work."

And I won't be plowing you at all. "Right. So, in other words, Brute and T.J. are pissed." Alarm bells started to ring when he broke eye contact. "Or maybe this is you backtracking. Again."

"No." His tone was harsh as their gazes met. "I'm not backtracking. I just need to figure some shit out."

He reached for her, and this time she went willingly into his arms, needing his touch. She didn't want to lose him this time. Even though her own emotions had her threatening to run at the thought of Vault of Sin, she didn't want to be rejected by him again. Not when she knew they could be great together.

"I'm serious about us. But T.J. and Brute made me realize there's a lot to lose if this doesn't work. We both need to appreciate what's at stake."

She could understand the need for caution. Hell, she had already come to terms with resigning from her job if things turned sour. What clenched her heart was his waning enthusiasm. After this afternoon, she'd expected to move forward with increased flirting and maybe more heated moments in more secluded areas. Not the cold shoulder currently being shoved down her throat.

"I understand what's at stake."

He inclined his head. "Well, then take the time to contemplate what will happen in Vault of Sin. Not only as an employee, but how you will feel when you finally let me take you down there as my partner."

She shuddered at the image. The internet research she'd done on sex clubs during her days off hadn't bettered her opinion of the erotic scene. Every site had a different outlook, and none sat favorably. One even claimed most clubs ran like brothels, with all single females in attendance being paid sex workers to heighten the chance of men getting their money's worth. Distaste had accompanied her Google search. It hadn't stopped her fingers tapping the keys though. She spent hours reading through lurid information, searching for a place like Vault of Sin. Leo, Travis and even the woman who'd approached her in the bathroom had spoken of a respectful environment. One Shay could probably grow to enjoy. Yet, all the pages she found contained sleazy information more focused on male bragging rights.

"I know it won't happen for a while." Leo ran a hand through her loose hair and focused his gaze on her lips. "But it's better for you to determine you don't want to be part of the lifestyle now instead of becoming disgusted with yourself, or me, later."

She gave a jerky nod, wishing she could argue or rally against him and confidently say she was happy to move forward. Only her anxiety over sex in that sort of environment still plagued her. "Okay. So, the plan is to ignore each other until Saturday?"

"Like I said, I'll be in my office concentrating on orders and tax bullshit. I won't be ignoring you, but I doubt I'll see you either."

Another nod. She was the weaker party in this duo and the realization didn't sit favorably. Men usually fawned over her, clinging to every opportunity to smother her. Leo's ability to brush her away so easily was like a kick in her overly sensitized ovaries. The grass definitely didn't seem so crisp on this side of the fence.

Time apart might be a good thing, though. It would give her space to strengthen herself against his appeal. It could even work in her favor, if he began to miss her. All she could do was hope he succumbed to the memory of her charms and came running for her before she did it first.

"No problem," she lied and retreated from his embrace. "I guess I'll see you Saturday then."

"Yeah."

She smiled through the disappointment and unlocked her car. "Bye."

He grabbed her hand as she made to leave and pulled her back into his arms. She had a second to catch her breath before his lips brushed hers, delicately sweeping and disappearing just as quickly.

She inwardly cursed her need to take things further, to run her hands under his shirt and mark his skin with her nails. Instead, she strode the remaining steps to her car, not bothering to wait for another farewell as she ignored the devil on her shoulder who chanted she'd just been ditched by Leo.

Again.

# CHAPTER FOURTEEN

S hay spent days *realizing what was at stake*. She thought getting through Tuesday to Thursday had been harrowing. Her body no longer ached from the sex high of the weekend. And the hours spent away from Leo, when he was only mere yards away, gave her doubts time to multiply. Yet, Friday night was worse.

She was working the main Shot of Sin bar, as usual, passing the time by trying to send Leo telepathic messages to come see her. Only he didn't. Not in the four hours since the club opened, or any other time during the past three days.

Her aggression had grown to a fever pitch. She was pissed off to the point of shaking, and no matter how hard she tried, she couldn't stop the ache in her chest demanding her to go in search of her damn annoying boss.

She didn't need space. She needed encouragement. Grounding. Maybe a little attention to relieve her apprehension. Now, after almost a week spent on the razor's edge of trepidation, she wasn't sure how she'd hold back her frustration when they finally did come face to face.

"Raspberry and vodka in a tall glass, please."

*You've got to be fucking kidding me.*

She ground her teeth at the same loner who came to her bar every damn week. He needed to learn that pretty pink drinks were never going to get him laid. Breathing deep, she grabbed a short glass from the tray, filled it and slid it toward him with a scowl.

"This isn't what I ordered." He frowned, raising his voice over the heavy bass music.

"No, it's not." Shay pointed to the scotch and dry in front of him. "This is what us bartenders like to call a man's drink." She paused, waiting for his ire. When none came, she smiled —all teeth and no charm. "That's all I'll be serving you from now on. So, drink up or find someone else to fill your order."

A scowl marred his usually smooth brow, yet he still handed over payment.

His inability to stick up for himself pissed her off even more. She was beyond frustrated. At the loner. At herself. And most of all, at Leo. He'd wrecked her, turning her into a pathetic, weak and second-guessing Nancy.

Her heart thumped in her chest. The strain from the previous week hit her with full force.

"I'm not finished." The words spilled out without her control. "You're also going to undo the top button of your straight-laced shirt, ruffle the fuck outta your nerdy hair, and for the love of God, walk around with a little pride. Stop sulking like you're handing over your balls every time you ask a woman if she wants a drink. You hear me?"

Her throat dried and her hands shook as she tried in vain to pull herself together. This was all Leo's fault. He was ignoring her. Flicking her away like a used candy wrapper. Not even sparing a moment to call, or send a freaking text message.

"Fucking asshole," she muttered and cringed when the customer's now angry gaze drifted past her shoulder.

"Shay."

She stiffened at the authoritative tone. *Christ*. The last thing she needed was Brute and all his heartless arrogance.

"Storeroom. Now," he growled.

She straightened her shoulders and swung around, not bothering to acknowledge her boss's existence before trudging away. As soon as they were alone in the small room, she began to crumple, her eyes burning with despised weakness.

"What's your problem?" he asked without inflection.

She didn't know how he contained himself. How he held all his feelings inside, never to be seen. Clearly, she didn't have his strength. "Nothing."

He raised a brow. That was all it took, a haughty, impatient brow telling her to hurry up and spill.

"You know I slept with Leo." There, she'd admitted it. Now she didn't have to pretend like her emotions weren't on the spin cycle anymore. Professionalism be damned, she was a woman with a bruised ego, everyone prepare for hysterics.

"Yeah, I know."

She waited, for something, anything, only he continued to stand there with his haughty brow.

"Well, he's avoiding me." She threw her hands up in frustration. "I'm introduced to all the secrecy downstairs, he comes to my rescue when some guy follows my car, he takes me home and fucks me silly, vowing he wants to be with me. Then all of a sudden, I don't exist."

She paused, hoping for comfort she knew better than to expect. The longer Brute remained quiet, the more worthless she felt.

"If he made a mistake, fine," she lowered her voice in defeat. "He just needs to tell me. Not to keep dragging me along for days. Man up and let me have it."

"I told him to give you space."

"You what?"

His gaze hardened, piercing her with annoyance. "I warned you a long time ago to stay away from Leo. You didn't listen, now you need to step back and realize what will happen when this doesn't work out."

When, not if.

"I'm aware I'll lose my job."

"Yeah. You will," he said without regret. "But what about Leo? What about Vault of Sin?"

She frowned, suddenly defensive. "What about it?"

"You're strong, Shay, but you're also a temperamental bitch at times, and quick to fly off the handle. If you leave here in a snit, how do we know you won't blab our secrets to the world?"

She jerked back as if he'd slapped her. "I wouldn't do that."

"Maybe not." He shrugged. "I'm not convinced you'd leave amicably though. Then there's Leo. He'll drop the ball at work, and T.J. and I will have to pick up the slack. It'll increase the popularity downstairs because he'll start plowing through the women like he's on death row, but it won't make my job easier."

Her heart shot to her throat at the image of Leo surrounded by a sea of naked women, all of them vying for his attention. "You're such a bastard."

"Just proving my point, sweetheart. You're the jealous type. And I think knowing he's currently downstairs at a private party would be enough to spark you into a rage."

The heart in her throat stopped beating and plummeted to the base of her stomach. "You're lying."

What had she done to deserve this from Brute? She'd always respected him, had even gone to him for advice because he didn't disguise the truth with bullshit. Finding out their friendship was a one-way street was another kick in the teeth.

"Why would I bother?" The lack of sentiment in his eyes told her he was telling the truth. "It's an intimate party and the host specifically requested Leo to be the overseer. Apparently, I'm not chummy enough with the patrons." He smirked, showing pride in his asshole reputation. "And T.J. isn't known for his participation."

Shay clenched her stomach to stop herself from doubling over. "He should've told me," she whispered. Leo had promised fidelity, and she would take him at his word, but picturing him surrounded by temptation and easy offerings made her second-guess everything—her confidence, her job, even their future together.

"He can't start asking you for permission to do his job."

She gulped in a breath and nodded. He was right. It didn't stop her feeling betrayed though. Leo had told her last week that she could never go downstairs without him. Would the demand ever run both ways?

"Shay." Brute softened his tone. "It's not too late to change your mind. Go home. Think things through. If you decide you don't want to be with him, then we'll shuffle the shifts around so you don't have to work together for a while. It'll blow over in no time, and work can go back to the way it's always been." He pinned her with his stare. "Things won't be as easy once the two of you become close."

"And what if I can't walk away?"

Brute looked at her with sympathy, the first heartfelt emotion she'd ever seen cross his face. "Then we all take it a day at a time."

She gave a derisive chuckle. "This isn't a group relationship."

He stood silent for a long moment, the heavy beat of bass echoing the thump of her heart. "You haven't thought this through, because you're not seeing the bigger picture. I don't think you realize what a life with Leo will mean."

"I'm sure I don't." He'd surprised her enough already. "But isn't my willingness to try a good indication of where my heart's at?"

"Go home, Shay. Picture your future with him from every angle." He stepped forward and briefly squeezed her shoulder. "And don't worry if you aren't ready for tomorrow night. If you don't show up, I'll know you need more time."

She rolled her eyes, trying to lessen the tension in the room. "You're just driving me away so you get to spend more time downstairs with the ladies."

"Sure am." He smirked, yet the jubilation quickly faded. "We don't want to lose you."

The sorrow in his voice cut deep, and finally she understood how a woman could've broken him so badly. "It's because of Vault of Sin, isn't it?" she spoke almost to herself. His harshness, the reaction to her being with Leo, it was all because of the way one of his previous lovers had treated him.

"What do you mean?" His voice regained its emotionless tone.

Shay gazed up into his blue eyes, noticing for the first time the tiny gray flecks around his pupils. She wanted to run a hand through the blond, chin-length hair combed back from his face and gently glide her palm along the light beard covering his chiseled jaw.

Without the damaged soul, he could be a gorgeous man. Only he wore his hatred like a shield, rarely smiling or softening the bitterness from his features. It would take a strong woman to heal him, and she hoped one day he would find her.

"Nothing."

He shrugged. "Okay. I'll let the rest of the staff know you're knocking off early."

She nodded as he turned to the door and slid it open. "Hey, Brute..."

He paused and glanced over his shoulder.

"You're not as heartless as you want us all to believe."

He laughed without humor. "Think what you like, sweetheart. But I assure you, I'm only looking out for myself."

Then he was gone, leaving Shay to shrink under the weight of her thoughts.

# CHAPTER FIFTEEN

*L*eo was pacing. Well, in reality he was sitting at the empty Vault bar, rubbing his forehead, wishing away his headache. But in his mind, he was climbing the walls. He couldn't stop. He was mentally exhausted, his body not equipped to handle this relationship bullshit.

Why did fucking someone on a regular basis have to be so complicated? He released a bark of laughter. If only this thing with Shay was mere fucking. But no, he had to go and get his emotions involved. He had to fall for her.

The last four days had been a nightmare. He'd sequestered himself in the back office, thinking the distance from the bar would make it easier for him to stay away. And it had been... until he'd remembered all the video feeds from the club could be accessed from his laptop. Then his working week had been shot to hell.

He'd watched her. For hours.

When the call for the private party had come through, he'd jumped at the opportunity to get away from his computer. Then he'd spent every hour downstairs wishing he was back behind his desk. Nothing took his mind off Shay, and now Saturday night had arrived, he wasn't sure how it would end.

A click sounded behind him, and he tilted his head to better hear the door opening from the main staircase. His heart beat in a crescendo, building with force until his chest pounded. He listened for the footfalls, hoping to hear the soft steps of Shay. He even held his breath, until the thudded stride informed him it wasn't the person he wanted.

"She's not here yet?" Brute asked.

Leo sighed and ran a hand down his face. "No. She's still got time though."

Last week, she'd said she'd arrive early, yet the seconds were ticking by. It was only forty-five minutes before guests would start to arrive.

Brute slid onto the stool beside him and stared straight ahead. "Don't hold your breath, buddy."

"Why?" Leo turned. "Do you know something I don't?"

"She snapped last night and took her anger out on one of the customers. I ended up sending her home early."

"Why wasn't I told?" He tried unsuccessfully to curb the steel in his tone.

"You were busy down here...which she didn't appreciate either."

Leo turned back to the bar, slowly counting the liquor bottles to stop himself from snapping. "You told her where I was?"

"Was I meant to lie?"

He lowered his head into his hands and sighed. "No. I just..." *Should've been the one to tell her.* "I want to see her." *I need her to show up.*

Christ. He had to shuffle on the stool to make sure he still had a dick between his thighs. He'd never cared this much for a woman. Not outside the bedroom, anyway.

"Look, man, I know you want this to work out, and so do I, but she doesn't have a clue about what to expect down here. I don't think she's even contemplated T.J. or my involvement."

"We were meant to be taking things slow. I didn't want to scare her off."

"Well, she'll be fucking frightened once she sees me naked. Ain't no woman gonna forget a package that big in a hurry."

Leo shook his head and grinned. "Too bad you don't know what to do with it."

"Sounds like jealousy, bro." Brute wiggled his fingers in Leo's ponytail.

"Fuck off." He slapped the hand away with a chuckle, yet the humor faded as fast as it arrived. His buddy was trying his best to cheer him up, and Leo appreciated it, only he'd been stuck in this sullen mood all week. Now time was running out, and his gut told him Shay wasn't going to show.

"I know I've been tough on you about this," Brute murmured into the quiet. "But I like Shay."

The hair on Leo's neck stiffened. His friend didn't admit to feelings. Ever. He didn't share or express affection. His admiration of women was only ever shown in the way his gaze raked their body, or how he went to great efforts to bring them pleasure. No words were ever spoken, because then they could be held against him.

"Stop bristling, lover boy. I'm not after your woman. I just wanted to keep an eye out for her. You strutted around the restaurant on Tuesday with your dick leading the way. I was hoping the days apart would give you both time to think clearly."

Leo released a painful breath. "My thoughts are as clear as they're gonna get, so can you let me take it from here now?"

"Sure thing." Brute slid from the stool. "I didn't push the

issue about the non-disclosure during the week. So I'll bring it down later in the hopes she turns up."

Leo nodded, not convinced she would. "Thanks."

"Keep your head up." Brute began to walk from the main room. "You look like a pussy when you mope."

~

*S*hay had been standing in the dim light above the back entrance to Vault of Sin for over ten minutes. She wasn't going to back out. Getting in the car to drive here had been the hard part. Only she wasn't entirely sure how to convince her finger to ring the bell on the control panel beside the door.

"This is work," she muttered to herself. "Nothing more."

Delusional much?

She may still be pissed off. Still angry as fuck at holding the weaker hand in whatever sexed-up game they were playing. But she was here for Leo. Plain and simple. Her cloying feelings for him were too strong to ignore.

No matter how many times she contemplated the worst-case-scenario outcome—the loss of her job, the hit to her confidence and the possible risk of utter humiliation—her heart continued to thump in a yearning beat. She needed Leo, and she was here to take a chance on any possible future with him. No matter how freakishly scary it was.

"Now you just have to press the goddamn button." She raised a shaky hand, held her breath and rammed her fingertip into the bell.

She ignored the small camera panel above the button and lowered her gaze to the shiny black heels she wore. Inwardly, she cursed herself for getting dressed up for tonight's shift. Her bartender uniform consisted of a Shot of Sin tank, which she currently wore. But instead of the three-quarter casual pants or jeans she normally donned, she was wearing a fucking skirt and her finest underwear. It had taken a truckload of chocolate to pull the lacy shit up her legs, and even more to clasp the Wonderbra behind her back. And she'd done it for him—the guy who'd ignored her all week.

The thick, steel-plated door creaked open, making her heart stop, and Leo came into view in his black pristine pants and another freshly ironed shirt. His lips were a thin line, lacking emotion, yet his eyes blazed with something she didn't want to determine. If he was angry she was a little late, he would have to deal with it.

He stood in silence, his gaze slowly raking her from head to toe and back again. Memories of last weekend heated her cheeks and she dulled the sudden spark of arousal with annoyance.

"Nice to see you again," she spoke over the lump in her throat.

His jaw stiffened, his nostrils flared, and right when she thought he was about to put her in her place, he grabbed her wrist and yanked her inside, pushing her against the wall as he slammed the door shut with his fist.

"Leo—"

He cut off her protest with his lips, devouring her mouth, claiming her before the darkened staircase. After a week without him, she couldn't maintain her anger. Her defenses crumpled, and she clung to him, kissing him back with equal fervor. His tongue entered her mouth, sliding against hers, drawing a moan from her throat.

This was what she wanted. Leo. Nothing else. No complications or expectations. Just him and her, together, enjoying one another. Then reality overcame her hormones and she remembered the distance he placed between them after every time they were intimate. She whimpered as she mustered the strength to nudge him away.

"Don't." She touched her lips with the tips of her fingers to stop them tingling.

"Shay." He reached for her with anguish etched across his features.

"You've been ignoring me."

He sighed and ran a rough hand through his hair, loosening the ponytail. "I told you, I was giving you time. And I owed it to T.J. and Brute to take this seriously. A lot is at stake."

"And what was I owed?" She'd never sounded so fragile, her voice had never been so weak, yet she couldn't strengthen her tone.

"The time to make up your own mind without me clouding your judgment." He leaned against the opposite wall, his focus never leaving hers. "I don't want to hurt you."

"You were hurting me all week."

"That wasn't deliberate. I've fucking missed you, Shay." He pushed from the wall and bridged the distance between them to rest his pelvis against hers. "If you knew how hard this week has been for me, you wouldn't still be shooting daggers my way."

"You set the distance rule, so you kinda deserve it." She softened her stare and gave him a weak smile. "Look, I know this will never be a conservative relationship. I've spent days coming to terms with that. But I'm here aren't I?" She wriggled out from underneath him and took the first few steps backward, needing space to remain clearheaded.

"They want you to sign a non-disclosure." He spoke as if it was the end of the world, waiting for her to become offended.

"Of course."

He narrowed his gaze and followed her. "You're unpredictable, you know that?"

She slid farther along the wall, sensing the heat radiating off him. "I aim to please."

His predatory focus honed in on her eyes as he closed in on her, leaning her into the cold plaster. "And you deliberately wore a skirt to tempt me, didn't you?"

*Yes.* "No. Not at all."

He laughed softly against her neck. "You're a seductress." He pulled back and rested his head against hers. "If you walk away, I'll respect your wishes. I won't chase you. But as long as you're here, I'm not going to be able to keep my hands off you."

She sucked in a breath at his raw possession. She itched to run her fingers under his shirt, to grind against the hardness in his pants. But the slightest touch would spark a fire she couldn't sate, and she didn't need to lose focus now. Not when she was meant to be working. "You need to increase your bipolar meds."

The side of his lips quirked as he pressed his erection into her abdomen. "You need to tame that sassy mouth."

"Or maybe you need to do it for me." She bit her lip, wishing she hadn't taunted him. "Come on. You need to show me around." This was going to be a tough night if she was the one who had to push away his advances. All week it had been the opposite, and she had no clue which dynamic she preferred. Chasing a gorgeous man was common sense. Pushing him away was plain idiocy.

She ducked under his arm and continued down the hall, around the corner and came out at the side of the bar. The empty room seemed different in the harsh fluorescent light and the scent of sex no longer permeated the air.

Leo groaned behind her and followed her into the open space. "Fine. But just so you know, I plan on following you home again tonight."

Shay kept her back to him, hiding her smile.

"We'll start over here."

She glanced over her shoulder and then turned to follow him into the first room along the side wall. She remembered it from last Saturday. The one with the large bed center stage.

Leo flicked on the light switch, and the tiny bulbs above the focal point twinkled to life. "My favorite room."

She remembered the threesome from last week with vivid clarity. The way the men had caressed the woman with loving affection. Shay could still see them on the mattress, their legs tangled, their smiles bright.

"You obviously already know about the bathrooms." He strode forward, pushed open the ladies door and reached inside to flick on the lights. Then he did the same with the males. "We've got cleaners who change the linens and restock supplies. If you ever work down here again, all you have to do is adjust all the lighting. But either myself, T.J. or Brute will always be down here to help." He strode past her to click on the bedside-table lamps.

"And what's your role down here," she asked.

He paused as he opened a drawer, and glanced over his shoulder. "Supervisor. Confidant. Sometimes instigator. Our role is to make sure everyone is comfortable and that no issues arise." He raised a brow, waiting for her response.

Instead of voicing her opinion, she nodded and focused on the items in the drawer.

"The bedside tables are filled with necessities, too— restraints, vibrators, lube. Condoms are used on the toys for hygiene reasons, but they're also sterilized after every party."

Shay winced and withheld a shudder.

He slammed the drawer shut and walked to her. "Come on. You don't need to see the rest. I'll help you set up behind the bar before everyone arrives." He grabbed her hand in a gentle grip and led her back into the main room. He rubbed his thumb along her skin as they walked in silence, and her heart galloped at the simple gesture from a man more accustomed to sexual moves than sweet ones.

"You still good with this?" He flicked off the fluorescent light beside the entrance to the bar and turning on the mood lighting.

"I'm good." Her voice was too chipper, too unrealistic.

He slowed to a stop, turned to face her and backed her into the counter behind the bar. His lips tilted, his eyes dancing in the darkness. "You're shitting yourself."

She rolled her eyes at his attempt to put her at ease. "Well, not literally."

"There's the sass I was looking for."

"I thought you wanted me to leash my sassiness?" She raised a brow in defiance.

He leaned closer, licking his bottom lip. "It's endearing in an annoying sort of way."

"I could say the same about you."

His grin continued to grow as he bridged the distance between them and brushed his mouth against hers. "That fucking perfume is driving me wild."

Score one to Calvin Klein.

His lips were forceful as his tongue entered her mouth. He played with her, coaxing her into murmurs of lust, making her clench her thighs together. He grasped her hips, lifted her onto the counter beside the beer taps and spread her knees apart. Then he slid his hands up her thighs, under her skirt and lowered her lace G-string.

It was too much. Too quick. Lust suffused her veins. Heat invaded her limbs.

"*Leo.*" She pulled back to brace her hands on the cool counter top as she sucked in ragged breaths.

"We're alone." He bent to untangle the underwear now at her feet and threw them onto the bar. "No one will walk in."

He lowered his zipper and raised her blood pressure at the

same time. She peered down at the enthusiasm tenting his boxers and bit her lip. He was impressive. More than impressive. He was orgasmic. And she was already wet for him, the tingling sensation between her thighs growing with every second.

"Come here." He grabbed her ass, pulling her to hover on the counter edge. He riffled through his pocket and pulled out a condom.

"Do you always have those on standby?"

"I will when I'm around you."

"Good answer." She watched him sheath himself, all that delicious male cock covered in dark blue and ready for her.

"Fast and hard, Shay. You ready?" He inched her off the bar, holding her in mid-air.

A grin tilted her lips. She loved the way he took charge. "Uh huh."

She clung to his shoulders and stifled a moan when he sunk home, just the way he promised. Quick and harsh. Needy and determined. Her core stretched around him with the slightest pleasure-filled ache.

It was forceful loving. Or fucking. She didn't know the difference, but he drove into her with powerful thrusts, the veins in his neck protruding, the muscles under her hands tightening.

He fucked her against the bar, consuming her with his efficiency, each movement hitting the exact spot necessary to nudge her pleasure into uncharted territory. The sound of skin slapping against skin filled the empty room, followed by her commands for more and his mindless groans. She wrapped her legs around his hips, demanding more, pulling him deeper until her throat went dry and her breasts ached to be touched.

"Fuck. You feel..." He closed his eyes and his nostrils flared as he panted.

Was he equally mindless? It didn't seem possible. He was experienced. Controlled. In contrast, she'd never had sex in a public place. Had only ever been touched by him in a storeroom.

The thought of being caught sent a wicked thrill down her spine, along each nerve, to throb in her pussy. This was all new. All pure fulfillment. She didn't want to let him go. Couldn't contemplate the thought of this ending. Yet, her core began to pulse with a building storm she'd never experienced so quickly.

"Holy shit." She was going to come and she'd barely kissed the man.

"You with me?" He opened his eyes, resting his head against hers as he continued to grind into her.

"God, yes." She was close enough to see black spots in her vision.

He leaned her against the bar, a hand grasping the back of her neck, his other arm holding her close. He started to move in rhythm. Thrust after deep-seated thrust, until she was digging her nails into his flesh, her mouth begging to be kissed.

He fulfilled her wish, taking her lips with harsh pressure, making her chest fire into a ball of uncontainable lust. She began to cry out in climax and he growled in response, following her over the edge.

Her back fought with the bar, her thighs clenched around his waist, her heart beat in a frantic pace of love, lust and fascination. Every part of her was consumed with him. Tuned to him. Hooked to only him.

The heavy slapping sounds lessened, the pounding rhythm died into a gentle embrace. She leaned back, meeting his stare and wondered how it had taken them so long to find something so natural.

Leo was what she needed.

He was the man to give her excitement, passion and pleasure.

He was the one who could keep her on her toes.

All she had to do now was convince herself this could work.

# CHAPTER SIXTEEN

"*D*on't stare at me like that," Leo whispered, the dark ruby of her lips making him want her all over again.

"Like what?" She loosened her grip on his shoulders and stroked the side of his face with a finger. For someone so tough and opinionated, she had a soft heart.

"Like you're offering me your soul." Her brown irises were still dark with lust, her mouth tilted toward his, willing, waiting. "I'll take it, Shay. And I'll never give it back."

Her lips curved, a delicate, almost embarrassed smile hitting him full force. They were on the same wavelength, held the same desire. In the end, passion would win. He knew it would.

"You can—" She gasped at the click of an opening door behind them. "Shit."

She shoved at his chest, pushing him until she had room to slide off the counter. Heavy footfalls came from the entry, while Shay rushed to straighten her skirt and untangle her hair.

"It's only T.J. or Brute." He took his time disposing of the used condom. "Nobody else is allowed down here yet."

She shot him a look of incredulity. "*Exactly*."

His heart changed from the desire-ridden thump to something rough, something uncomfortable. They had so many things to discuss, and no time to do it. Later, once the club was closed and he'd taken her home to sate their lust, they'd talk. And they wouldn't stop until all cards were on the table.

She needed to understand his sex life was intertwined with T.J. and Brute's. They weren't gay, had never even glanced down that path, but they shared a lot of sexual moments, and many, many women. It was like an additional partnership added to their business relationship. The three of them knew how to work together, to make a woman wild and replete. Even though T.J. didn't participate physically, he still played an integral role, and contemplating the conclusion of this part of Leo's life was like a stab through his gut.

Shay was strong and he could sense her curiosity for Vault of Sin. But no matter how much she lessened the tight hold on her inhibitions, Leo doubted she would ever be able to participate with all her bosses around to enjoy the show.

Brute strode into the room, clearing his throat in a less than subtle manner. "Catch you at a bad time?" he drawled, hitting Leo with an unapologetic smirk. A silent message of congratulation passed between them, one that Leo acknowledged with a slight tip of his head.

Shay's back stiffened and she spun around to face the interloper. "Just setting up for the night."

Leo tried not to laugh at her high-pitched tone and placed a strong hand at the low of her back. "Chill," he whispered in her ear.

"Right." Brute raised a brow as he slid across a stool and

stretched his arm over the bar. "You might need these then." He retrieved her lace G-string from the counter and held it up on his pointed finger.

She sucked in a breath, the back of her neck and sides of her cheeks turning pink. If it had been any other woman, Leo would've assumed she was embarrassed, only Shay's balled fists below the counter said otherwise.

"Thanks," she gritted through clenched teeth and snatched her underwear from Brute's hold. "I'm going to freshen up." She strode around the counter, head held high, spine straight, and left the room without another word.

Leo waited until she was out of view before he turned to Brute. "Was that necessary?"

"Yeah. Kinda." The smug fucker still flashed a tiny grin. "Thanks for the show. Obviously, you didn't hear me open the door the first time. I had to go back and pretend I was coming in again."

Leo narrowed his gaze. Normally, Brute wouldn't have given a shit about interrupting. He would've pulled up a stool and watched without remorse. "It's not like you to walk away from me putting on a show."

"It's not you I watch, asshole. My focus is always on the women, and this is different. This is Shay."

Shit. Had he fucked up by assuming his friends wouldn't mind her involvement in Vault of Sin? They hadn't brought it up, but neither had they discussed it. "And you don't want to watch her?"

"If I had a problem with her participating down here, I would've spoke up sooner. I just thought you guys were still on shaky ground and I didn't want to rock the boat."

Leo released the breath tightening his lungs. "Thanks."

"Relax. She turned up. That was the hardest part." The arrogance returned to Brute's face. "And for future reference,

I'd watch her all damn day. In fact, I'd be happy to show her what she's missing not being with a real man."

Leo rolled his eyes. "No point baiting me. I'm wound too tight to snap back. You're more likely to score a fist to the throat."

"I actually thought Shay might've done the same when I was swinging around her panties." Brute chuckled. "That woman is going to keep you on your toes."

Damn straight. "Yeah. If this works out, she'll send me gray before my time." Leo couldn't wait.

"And what will it take for this to work? She was pretty freaked when I walked in. Are you willing to change your extra-curricular activities to keep her?"

Leo glanced toward the door Shay had disappeared into and rubbed a hand along the stubble of his chin. "I don't know. I'm going to try whatever necessary, and she's trying, too. It's a hell of a lot further than any of us have traveled with this fucked up lifestyle."

A bitter tinge entered Brute's gaze. "True. Just remember the higher you get, the harder you fall."

"I don't plan to fall."

"Good." Brute slid from his stool. "I'm happy for you both." He reached behind his back and pulled a folded piece of paper from his pocket. "The non-disclosure." He handed it over. "Make sure she reads it before you shove your dick into her again. We don't want her claiming she had to sign under duress."

The faint squeak of the bathroom door sounded as Leo snatched the paper. "If you walked in on us before, you'd know there was no duress. Just a gorgeous woman who happens to enjoy my handiwork."

Brute scoffed. "Yeah. Too bad for her, your personality isn't as endearing."

"As endearing as what?" Shay strolled toward them, one eyebrow raised.

"Nothin'." Leo strode around the bar, fighting the need to surge forward and claim her again. "Brute was just leaving."

# CHAPTER SEVENTEEN

*S*hay was proud she'd kept her cool for most of her shift. She served partially dressed patrons with ease, even fought the impulse to stare at the appendages of the entirely naked ones, and she no longer felt the cloying discomfort whenever her gaze brushed past sex scenes in the main room.

In fact, she was beginning to enjoy watching, a little too much. Her G-string was uncomfortably soaked, and every time Leo walked into view, she cursed the way her nipples tingled. It was worse when he came to check on her. She ached to grab his shirt collar and drag him into the storeroom.

But that wasn't how things worked down here. Everything was about exhibitionism, not hiding in storage closets and making out in the dark. More importantly, it wasn't what Leo desired. As the minutes ticked by, her motivation to give him what he wanted increased. So did the nervousness.

"Can I order a juice, please?"

Shay smiled at the petite brunette and nodded. "Sure."

Another thing she loved was the professional manner in

which everyone interacted. The cost of entry downstairs included free alcohol, yet none of them rushed to get their money's worth. Everyone played it cool, keeping level-headed. The perception of a seedy sex club was entirely different from the reality of Vault of Sin.

Shay handed over the juice and tingled with the brush of someone's gaze on her skin. She turned her head and found Leo watching her, his eyes glazed with lust. Her focus lowered to his crotch and she shuffled uncomfortably at the thickness pressed against his zipper.

*Whore.*

She smiled to herself. Yep, her thoughts were those of a bona fide slut, and she didn't give a rat's ass. She'd never been so aroused in her life. And right now, she didn't care what was turning Leo on. All she wanted was to sate their cravings.

As she continued to serve polite patrons, she watched him mingle in the main room. He put those who appeared nervous at ease. Always remaining the professional host with his confident posture and commanding stare, all the while glancing at her every few minutes with irises that never ceased making her burn.

To stop herself from escaping to the bathroom for her own private play session, she turned her back to the room and began wiping down the shelf filled with high-class liquor bottles.

"Leo."

The purred feminine call had Shay snapping round on her heels. The petite brunette she'd served earlier was now draped around Leo, both arms wrapped around his neck with a familiarity that flicked Shay's jealous-bitch switch.

The only thing between the attractive woman and the boner Shay wanted to grapple was two thin layers of clothing. *Keep calm. You can't stab people.* She swung back around, trying to curb her inner bitch by keeping busy, and accidentally nudged a bottle of lime-flavored syrup off the counter.

*Fanfuckingtastic.*

"Shay, are you all right?" Leo called, his voice more authoritative than concerned.

"Peachy." She chanced one last look at him and the leech hanging from his neck before she grabbed a dust pan from under the counter and began cleaning the sticky mess.

So much for her keeping her cool. Her eyes were burning and palms sweating with the need to start her first cat fight.

Just imagine what it will be like next week when you're working back upstairs and unable to keep an eye on him. Shay growled. Was it always going to be like this—peaks of arousal followed by consuming lows depressing enough to make her needy and weak?

"This sucks."

Surely there was something she could do to turn the tables. It wasn't about claiming him in front of a crowd. It was about feeling secure and confident again. It was about regaining her strength. She just wasn't sure how.

~

*E*very muscle in Leo's body was tense as he tried to keep his erect cock from rubbing against Grace. There was only one woman causing the current pubescent reaction to his body, and the sassy little wench was probably muttering a curse under her breath, hoping his eager appendage would fall off. Yet, he couldn't bring himself to ditch the woman before him just to sate Shay's unease.

It was a tough line to draw, but this was life in the Vault of Sin. He would never dishonor a monogamy vow. Ever. However, in the past he'd been intimate with more than one of the women participating tonight, and he wouldn't alienate them by brushing them aside.

It was still his job to make everyone comfortable within these sordid walls, and as long as he wasn't reciprocating any sexual advances, he wasn't doing anything wrong.

"You're stiff," Grace murmured.

No shit. He was hard as stone.

Grace giggled to herself. "I mean your posture. What's wrong?" She released her arms from his neck and met his gaze.

"I'm fine. Just a little out of sorts tonight." He glanced toward the bar. Shay rose to her feet with the dustpan in hand and shot him a scowl before breaking eye contact.

"Ouch." Grace followed his line of sight. "Your new bartender doesn't look happy."

He released a grunt of frustration and shook his head. Shay looked like she wanted to flay him alive.

"She's gorgeous though."

"Yeah." There was no denying it. "She is."

"Oh, damn." Grace took a step back and tilted her head to meet his line of vision. "Did I cause that? Are you two together?"

Leo struggled to paste on a smile and met Grace's gaze. "It's okay. I don't think either of us know what we're doing at the moment."

"She's not into girls, is she?" Grace grinned and waggled her brows.

Fuck. His dick pulsed, fighting with the zipper of his pants. He'd been down here too many times to have a hair-trigger cock, only the thought of Shay and Grace made his blood surge south. "She's not into the lifestyle."

His own words resonated, penetrating his cloud of arousal. This wasn't her scene. He was pushing her to change her ways. The exact thing he'd hated other women trying to do to him.

"Give her time. Apart from glaring at you with contempt, she doesn't seem to have an aversion to the club itself."

He nodded, gaining some comfort from the possibility of truth in her words. "Yeah. I'm trying." Only he didn't know how long he could stand back and let Shay move at her own pace. He was too eager to have her splayed before a crowd. To have others watch as her beautiful face contorted with release. To see her luscious breasts, smooth stomach and tight pink pussy moving in a dance to set them all on fire.

Yet, he'd drive himself insane with lust before he pushed her.

"Go to her." Grace jerked her head in the direction of the bar. "Give her my apologies. And if she's ever into a bit of girl-on-girl action, I call first dibs." She strode around him, slapping his ass hard enough to make him take a step forward.

Perfect timing. Shay hadn't missed the friendly tap. She stood tall with one hand tightly fisted around a mop handle. Her eyes were glittering and her cheeks flushed with spite. And he couldn't help acknowledging with a grin that she looked hotter than he'd ever seen.

Her nostrils flared as he made his way to the bar, instinctively staying on the customers' side so he didn't get a mop head to the balls. "I'd ask you how you're doing, but your facial expression says it all."

"I estimate you can see about a tenth of the emotion I currently feel." She scrunched her nose and sashayed her angry ass to the small storage room behind the bar.

He strode after her, the first time he'd ever chased a woman. Thankfully, she ditched the mop and made an attempt to push her way back to the bar., but he blocked the doorway with his body.

"Let it out." He blocked the doorway with his body. "Tell me what's making you want to claw my eyes out."

"Isn't it obvious?" She scowled. "I don't appreciate other women touching you. It's not something I think will ever change. And definitely not a scenario I want to imagine every time you're down here without me."

"You mean you can never get used to me rejecting attractive women so I can be with you? Because that's the way I see it." He stepped into her, grabbing her around the waist. "It will take time for everyone to know I'm no longer open to play. I'm not going to send out a fucking memo. So to some extent, you need to get over it."

She released a derisive laugh and shook her head in frustration.

"This isn't going to be the reason you walk away from me," he demanded. "This is the reason you're going to stick around. Because you'll soon realize you have what every other woman in here wants. Me."

"Arrogant much?"

He smirked and shrugged a shoulder. "Is it really arrogance if it's true?"

"*Yes.*"

He softened his features and brushed his lips against hers before she could pull away. "Grace told me to apologize to you. She realized why you were giving us the evil eye."

"Great." She stepped out of his embrace. "Now I'll be known as the jealous bar bitch."

"You play the part well."

Her eyes flared and he caught her wrist when she tried to slap his chest.

"Look." He chuckled. "I told her I was taken and she backed off. You should be happy. Even more so, that she then became more interested in seeing if you were into girl-on-girl action."

"What?" Her eyes widened.

"You heard me." He bridged the distance between them again, pushing them farther into the darkened storeroom, not giving a shit if patrons were waiting for bar service. "So should I be jealous?" He backed her into a wall, and leaned his body into hers. "Because I'm not. I'm hard as hell thinking about another woman going down between your pretty thighs."

# CHAPTER EIGHTEEN

*A* strangled noise escaped Shay's throat. Yet again, she was struggling to gain her footing.

Girl-on-girl action? Holy shit. She'd thought her days of experimenting had died with her teen years. Muff diving had never been on her fantasy list. Yeah, she'd shared a drunken kiss or two with friends, but that had been a lifetime ago. Only now, knowing she'd excite Leo by diddling another woman made another thrill shoot through her body.

"I need to get back to work," she rasped.

He chuckled, fucking chuckled in her ear before stepping back to let her leave. "I'll be calling last drinks soon. You should start worrying about what will happen once we get back to your place. I've got a week's worth of attention to dish out."

She increased her pace from the storeroom, needing space so her nipples didn't bore a hole through her bra. She'd wanted to be more sure of herself before she left Vault of Sin tonight. Because walking out of here would be easy, but coming back as a participant would be a nervous nightmare.

And after a lifetime of being confident in herself, she was damn sick of the apprehension.

She'd thought turning up tonight had been difficult, yet all her appearance had done was voice her willingness to be in a relationship with Leo. What she really needed to do was make a choice. Decide right here, right now, if she could be a part of this lifestyle. No fucking around for days. Or second-guessing what might or might not be. She couldn't wait around for a set of balls to miraculously appear between her thighs, she had to pull up those soggy, sexy lady underwear and bite the bullet. She didn't want to change the man she'd fallen for, so the question was, did she want to be with Leo on his terms, in his environment? Or say to hell with all the angst and take the easiest option for all of them, T.J. and Brute included, and simply walk away.

She sucked in a breath and ignored the stone settling in her chest. She adored Leo, always had, only things were much deeper now, and a great deal scarier. What if she gave Vault of Sin a try and her family found out? What if she choked, literally, and made a fool of herself? What if she wasn't good enough?

In reality, he was asking her to be a performer in the rawest way. And yeah, she owned her shit, but spreading her thighs to the world required a set of brass balls...and she didn't even own a plastic pair.

Leo strode past the bar, confident as always as he played the supervisor role. He was at home here in a club most people would cringe at. She was proud he owned his proclivities. Last week, she'd made a fool of herself by judging him without reason. Because glancing around the room, all she could see were happy faces. Everyone was having fun. Even those who sat in groups chatting, no orgasms required. The crowd was different from her previous visit. A completely new mass of faces, yet the atmosphere was the same.

Friends or strangers, they all seemed to be brought together by a familiar bond. They didn't snigger or walk off in small groups to pass judgment on others. It was a quaint group of friends having a party. Only instead of playing cards and getting drunk, people got naked and played with each other.

The lifestyle here wasn't seedy or sleazy. There were no men lurking in the corners, or women playing mind games. It was sex in a safe environment. Simple as that.

"Last drinks," Leo raised his voice to vibrate through all the rooms.

"Oh, shit." Shay felt the color drain from her face.

This was it. She had two options. One would test her limits and may even break her, but the chance of happiness would accompany the journey. While the other road was easy, only she'd walk the smooth, stone path alone.

"Bloody hell," she muttered to herself. There was no way she could find the answer tonight. Not without hard liquor. And there was no chance of getting up close and personal with Mr. Grey Goose while working and having to drive home later.

Fate had got her this far...along with a little stubbornness. It looked like a flip of the coin would have to do.

~

*L*eo had called last drinks a few minutes early because Shay's complexion was becoming paler with every passing moment. He didn't want to contemplate the look in her eyes or what she planned on telling him the next time they were alone. So he kept himself busy and said farewell to the patrons who began to leave.

T.J. and Brute would've already closed Shot of Sin and be in the process of packing up for the night. He just hoped to fuck they didn't make their way downstairs looking to play while Shay was still around.

He knew she was slowly coming to terms with strangers fornicating around her, but he doubted she had grasped the concept of T.J. and Brute being involved. Or maybe she had in the last hour and that was why all the color had vanished from her skin.

"Good luck with your bartender." Grace came up to him, now dressed in a tight black cocktail dress with a purse clutched in one hand and a set of keys jangling in the other. She leaned in and placed a gentle kiss on his cheek. "Give her time. I know you haven't had the best experience with the ladies, but go easy on her. Adapting to new sexual experiences is more emotional for women. We tend to hold tight to our bad choices and analyze things to the point of insanity."

"Thanks," he muttered and then cringed at his rudeness. "I might see you next week," he lied. It was highly doubtful with the way things were heading with Shay. If he had to make a prediction, he'd say his time in the Vault was drawing to an end, at least for a while.

He walked away, heading for the entrance to turn off the large flat-screen. All he wanted was to get out of here. Which was fucking ironic, because all his problems with Shay stemmed from his need to be in Vault of Sin in the first place.

When he strode back into the main room, only three guys and two women remained, finishing their drinks as they lounged on one of the king-sized beds. His gaze sought Shay's, but she was gone. His head snapped around to do a quick visual sweep of the area—not in the bar, the storeroom door was closed and he doubted she was in any of the private rooms.

*Shit.*

He'd made a mistake earlier. He promised he wouldn't chase her if she ran. Hell. He didn't even know if she'd left and already he was fighting the need to kick everyone out so he could find her. His palms began to sweat as he pounded out the steps to the bar. Once he was behind the counter, he rushed to the cabinets under the sink and huffed out a relieved breath. Her handbag was there. She hadn't run. Not yet.

He climbed to his feet and checked the storeroom. Empty. He locked it behind him and went to the first private room filled with numerous beds. Again, no sign of her, so he flicked off the light and shut the door.

That only left one place to check, unless she was upstairs. He stood in the doorway of his favorite room and stared at the mattress bathed in light. Yesterday, he would've given anything to see Shay lying atop the black sheets. Now, he'd give anything to have her in his arms, simply holding her in the quiet of his apartment. Could he forego his current need to participate and live a life without Vault of Sin? Maybe. He would at least try. For Shay.

He flicked off the light, killing his fantasy with a sharp click and turned his attention to the ladies bathroom door as it squeaked open.

"Shay?"

She came to him with her head held high. In the dim light emanating from the main room, he could see the uncertainty in her eyes, right before she reached on her toes to kiss him. It was soft, sweet, entirely opposite to the ball-busting woman he knew, and his heart ached all the more for her.

His hands found her hips and he slid his tongue into her willing mouth as her warmth filled his chest. When she pulled back, he was no longer uncertain. He knew what he needed in his sex life and it wasn't other peoples' lust. It was Shay.

Only Shay.

She met his gaze with a half-smile, half-wince marring her face. Slowly, she raised her hands to the hem of her shirt and, with a deep, unsettling breath, raised the material over her head and let it fall to the floor.

*Fuck me.*

"There's people still out there." He glanced over his shoulder to make sure they were alone.

She gave a shaky nod and lowered her skirt to pool at her feet. "I know." She stood before him in black lace, the firm mounds of her breasts plumped and begging to be touched.

"*Shay.*" He swallowed over the dryness in his throat. She needed to put her clothes back on and walk from the room. Now. He didn't have the restraint to maintain the distance between them for too much longer. "What's this about?"

She sucked in a strengthening breath and climbed onto the bed, laying her delicious curves down in the middle of the mattress. "This is me, risking humiliation, to give myself to you."

He held back from pouncing, from taking what he wanted and instead rubbed a hand over the rough stubble at his jaw. Grace's words repeated in his mind. *"Adapting to new sexual experiences is more emotional for women. We tend to hold tight to our bad choices and analyze things to the point of insanity."*

This was too quick for Shay.

"Don't get me wrong, but why now? You're not ready for this."

Her face was shadowed in the darkness as she rested back on her elbows. "I'm taking a leap. I don't want to spend weeks stressing over what will happen. I want to do this now and have my answer straight away."

He stepped forward and rested his knees against the side of the bed. "What's the question?"

She paused, leaving them in heated silence for long

moments. "I want to know if I can be enough for you."

His nostrils flared with a sudden burst of anger. He wanted to spank her ass and prove to her in many pleasurable ways just how compatible they were. "You're enough," he growled. No other woman had set his heart racing like she did.

"Then show me." She sat up and moved toward him on her knees. "Do with me what you will, and if we both make it through to the other side, maybe we'll have a chance of taking this further."

His body tensed from his chest to his toes as she ran her hands over his pecs to grab the collar of his shirt. She tugged him forward and he followed her onto the mattress, crawling between her parted thighs as she scooted back to the top of the bed.

She loosened his ponytail with a hand through his hair, making the chin length strands curtain their faces. "You're quiet," she whispered against his lips, her breath heating every inch of him.

"I'm worried."

She pulled back into the pillows and frowned up at him. "But I thought—"

"There's only two possible outcomes to this. Either we'll be perfect for each other..."

"Or I'll have to quit my job if things go wrong."

He nodded. Shay was a passionate woman with a mean jealous streak. Working together after a botched relationship wouldn't be an option. And as much as his dick was willing to take the chance, a dull throb behind his ribs made him proceed with caution. "We can save this for another day."

She remained still beneath him, her chest rising and falling against his. When her hand fell from his hair, he anticipated her moving out from beneath him, to leave and rethink her decision. Then she swept her fingertips over his jaw, his chin and finally his lower lip before her mouth brushed his.

"I'm willing to risk it."

~

*S*hay waited with her heart in her throat and her confidence slowly fading. Leo continued to stare at her in the dim light, his quiet breathing the only thing she heard over the murmured voices in the next room.

People were out there, sipping drinks without a care while she lay in her underwear beneath a man she began to pray would say something.

"If we do this, I won't be quiet, and I won't allow you to hold in your pleasure," he warned. "We'll have an audience before my clothes hit the floor."

She swallowed. "I know."

He went silent again, and finally she appreciated the time he took to take the next step. His cock was hard between them, the thick length pressing against her pubic bone. He wanted her, yet he was proceeding with caution. Weighing up the pros and cons like she had for so long.

"I'll push you, Shay." He leaned in to gently slide his tongue along her bottom lip and his hand down her side to brush the curve of her breast. "I don't know any other way in here."

"I know." She shuddered, part of her wanting to be pushed while the other hoped adrenaline would see her through to the end without fleeing.

"Then take off your clothes." He pushed one cup of her bra up to expose her breast and leaned down to lap her nipple with his tongue. "I want every inch of you at my disposal."

She arched her back and swung her arms behind her to unclasp the hooks of her bra. As she slid the straps down, he lavished her with attention, licking one and then the other until her inhalations became labored and her skin tingled with sensitivity.

"Tell me you want me."

"I want you," she whispered, thrusting her breast into the heat of his mouth, dying under the touch of his fingers as they travelled along her waist.

"Louder."

Her heart thumped beneath her chest. "I want you." Her voice rose with each word, her adrenaline spiking with it.

He chuckled and pulled back to look her in the eye. "That meek voice does shit for my ego. Tell me you want me like you mean it. Like the tough girl I know you are."

She bit her lip, staring him down in determination, her nostrils flaring in spite. He raised a brow and skidded his fingers over her abdomen, slipping under the waistband of her G-string.

"Giving up already?" He flicked her clit, making her jolt.

"No. Just give me a second to prepare myself."

"No more thinking," he growled. "Say it." He parted her folds with his fingers and penetrated her in one delicious thrust. "Say it now."

"Jesus Christ," she wailed. "I want you, Leo."

He flashed her a predatory smile before sliding his touch from her body. "That's better." He gripped her G-string on either side of her hips and yanked the flimsy material down her legs.

She hoped the blood rushing through her ears was the only reason the soft murmuring in the next room had stopped. Not that they had fallen quiet to listen. Either way, she was determined to ignore any stranger who wanted to catch an eye full. This was her time to prove herself to the man she'd been dreaming about, and she definitely needed to lift her game.

She reached for his shirt and began to undo his buttons, unable to pull her gaze away from the skin she continued to expose. His chest was covered in a light dusting of hair, his pecs defined, his abs smooth and taut. She ached to run her hands along the lines of sinew, to bite into his flesh and make him flinch. She wanted to make him mindless, to repay him for the way he'd made her feel for too damn long.

With a rough hand, he pushed apart her thighs, exposing her, making her more vulnerable than ever before. She was on display, at his mercy, and her body had never felt more alive.

"You'll always be open for me. You understand?"

Her legs trembled as she undid his last button with shaky hands. "Yes," she murmured. "Always."

"And you will only ever give yourself to me."

She lowered her hands to her sides and raised a brow. "As long as the same rules apply to you."

"Always." He grinned, boosting her confidence even though the threat of other beautiful women from Vault of Sin hovered in the back of her mind.

"This is mine." He glided his hand over her abdomen and then lower. She pressed her lips together to fight a mewl when he slid two fingers through her dripping sex. He leaned over her, his hand still on her pussy while the other palmed her breast. "These are mine."

She whimpered, thrusting her chest into his hand. "Yes." She moved her hands to the bedhead and gripped the wooden frame, digging her nails into the timber. "Please, Leo."

He held her gaze, slowly gliding his fingers into her sheath as she released a long, deep moan. He withdrew just as languorously and wiped a trail of her juices around her clit, flicking the bundle of nerves back and forth. Movement came into her periphery and she froze, sensing more than one person hovering in the doorway.

"Focus on me," Leo demanded.

She tried. Really, she did, but the pleasure in her body began to ebb and all she could see were the shadows of onlookers darkening her lover's features.

"Me, Shay."

He yanked off his shirt and threw it to the mattress beside her. The hard, unyielding flesh was enough to distract her for a fleeting moment. Then her gaze drifted, moving to the couple standing close together against the wall, then to the two familiar faces in the open doorway.

"Holy shit." She grabbed Leo's shirt to cover her exposed breasts as she squeezed her eyes shut.

T.J. and Brute were there, watching her like a fucking porn show, their focus harsh enough to burn a lasting impression on her retinas.

"Close the door," Leo ordered, making her wince at the disappointment in his tone.

She'd wanted to impress him, to wipe away every memory he had of other women, and replace them with the crazy passion she had to share. How the heck had T.J. and Brute skipped her attention? Travis had mentioned staff participating after last drinks, yet the important point hadn't crossed her mind. She shook her head at herself as shuffled footsteps drifted into the distance and the door closed with a click.

Then the back of her eyelids were illuminated with the overhead lights and her eyes burst open.

*Don't panic. Don't freak out...any more than you already have.*

"Aren't they meant to be on the other side of the door?" She clung tighter to the shirt, as T.J. and Brute approach the bed.

"Calm down."

Calm down? She was crazy with panic. Hadn't they just discussed remaining faithful, albeit vaguely? Now T.J. stood to the left of the bed, his somber smile focused her way as if he was about to face a firing squad instead of a naked woman. Then there was Brute. His usual scowl had deepened, his eyes harsh with disapproval.

"Yeah, calm the fuck down, Shay," she muttered. "How the hell am I meant to do that with him glaring at me?" She flicked her gaze to Brute before swallowing over the emotion building in her throat and then focused on the black cotton sheets.

This was a fuck up of epic proportions.

"I suppose now would be an inappropriate time to ask for a glowing reference."

"I'm not letting you run," Leo spoke softly. "Look at me."

When she didn't, he made a move to climb off her. On instinct, she gripped him around the neck and yanked him back down.

"I'm naked," she ground through clenched teeth. "Move off me and die."

"I won't, if you look at me." He settled between her thighs and leaned on one elbow to peer down at her.

*Fine.* She raised her gaze, coming face-to-face with penetrating ocean eyes.

"You wanted to jump in the deep end, Shay. Don't forget how to swim now that you're here."

His words repeated in a continuous loop. Taking the plunge wasn't meant to be easy...it also wasn't meant to be this confronting, but if she walked away now, there was no way she would come back.

"I'm not in this for anyone else," she whispered. "All I wanted was you."

Her gaze drifted away, over the sheets to the dark blue jeans T.J. was wearing. He stood still, not uttering a word while Leo ran a finger along her jaw, regaining her attention.

"All you're getting is me. For however long you want me." He narrowed his gaze, hitting her hard with his sincerity.

"Playing with others would only be for your pleasure. And that doesn't have to happen now, or tomorrow, or ever. You got that?"

She nodded, slightly relieved at his statement.

"But my ego needs to be fed." The corner of his lips lifted, making her chest pound with his sexy confident smirk. "I want them to see your beautiful body. I want them to take notes on how fucking amazing I make you feel. I want their gaze on your face as you come undone by my hands, or my mouth, or my cock. I want them delirious with the need to have you."

She shuddered, feeling the exposed skin all over her body break out in shivering gooseflesh.

"Do you trust me?" he asked.

She bit her tongue to fight back the hell no. "Not when you're smirking like the cat that got the cream."

"But I do have the cream, gorgeous." His grin increased as he slid a hand between them, spreading her slick, sensitive flesh. "I just need you to trust me so I can get the chance to taste it."

Her breath hitched as he sunk his fingers deeper, gliding his thumb over her clit. "Okay," she gasped. "Okay." Okay, okay, okay. She nodded and licked her lips, dying for more. One touch was all she required to make her succumb. One touch and one wickedly sexy grin and she was all his.

"That's my girl."

He leaned in for a demanding kiss. His tongue penetrated her mouth with the same delicious rhythm of his fingers in her pussy. She clung to him, one hand around his neck, the other on his biceps, and let sensation take away her insecurities.

When he pulled back, she was panting, rocking her hips in need for more.

"T.J., get the cuffs."

"What?" Her gaze shot to T.J. at the bedside table to her left, then over to Brute who took a seat on the mattress to her right, before snapping back to Leo. "Cuffs aren't necessary." She shook her head, pleading with her gaze. She had too much pride to plead aloud. If they were alone it would be different, but she had to regain some level of backbone to prove to the others she was worthy.

"They are until you lose that frightened look in your eyes."

"I assure you, cuffs won't help."

T.J. softly chuckled and the impact of the sound stunned her. She glanced over to him, to the sweet gentleness in his wistful smile and knew she was safe. He had yearning in his eyes, just like Leo, and she supposed Brute had it somewhere too, under all those layers of brutality. They'd lost hope in finding the women to complete them and needed hope to move forward. She was that hope.

Silently, she raised her arm to T.J., letting the gentle touch of his hand work the cold metal around her wrist. He held her gaze as he locked it in place and then lightly ran his fingers from her wrist to her elbow before backing away to throw the other set of cuffs to Brute.

She didn't want to turn her gaze to the smug bastard. He'd had his fun with her underwear earlier. She could imagine how he would torment her once this moment was over. So instead of looking at him, she raised her arm in his direction and stared at Leo as an unfamiliar touch worked its way around her skin. Fingers tickled her wrist, working higher over her palm, spreading her fingers before moving back down again.

"He needs you to acknowledge his presence," Leo murmured.

Too bad. She raised her chin and worked her lower lip between her teeth, waiting for the delicate touch to end.

Brute was her friend, a great guy hiding behind an asshole persona. One glance could ruin the connection they had and she was already risking enough with Leo.

Leo chuckled. "Well, just so you know, he won't stop until he gets what he wants."

Her eyes widened as Brute's fingers continued to travel along her arm, from the tingling flesh around her elbow, to her biceps and finally her shoulder. She held her breath, wrapping her legs around Leo's waist for grounding, willing herself not to break.

Her skin burned in the wake of Brute's touch along her neckline, slowly down her sternum. She began to pant, caught between enjoying the lust wracking her body and the determination not to break so their relationship wasn't catapulted into another turbulent atmosphere.

"Shay," Brute's deep voice called.

She shook her head, fighting hard to calm herself.

"Shay." This time his voice was louder, and he drifted his fingers to the tingling flesh below her breast. "Look at me."

"Why?" She directed her frown at Leo. "You don't want me here." The truth escaped her lips. He'd warned her away from Leo when she was first employed and again last night. Subconsciously, his rejection had already cut deep.

"No." He let the force of his word sink in before he continued. "I don't want you hurt in here."

She looked at him then, at the way his scowl had softened into something like regret.

"I don't want to see you walk away like every other woman each of us have cared about."

That's not what their conversations had been about. Or was it? She scrutinized him, seeing the honesty in his features. Had his disapproval been out of protection for her?

"I'm a big girl."

He inclined his head. "I know, and that's why seeing you

so shaken is hard to take." His touch travelled over her ribs and then dropped from her side. "I'm here to protect you. To make sure this guy doesn't fuck up, okay?"

Her lips tilted. "Okay."

"I won't fuck up," Leo interrupted and pulled back from her body.

She winced at the exposure, sensing the weight of three heated gazes rake her from head to toe. Leo stood at the foot of the bed, devouring her with his eyes as he unclasped the button at his waistband, lowered his zipper and pushed his pants to the floor.

His erection tented the front of his boxers, making her mouth salivate, her restrained hands clench. He lowered the last piece of material covering his body and let his cock bob against his abdomen as he shucked his underwear.

"Time for the cat to get the cream," he drawled.

He fucking drawled at her with smooth male arrogance and then crawled back onto the mattress and parted her thighs. He had no inhibitions, no shyness, no doubt. He was in his element, his eyes alight with determination.

"Jesus Christ, you're beautiful." He sat back on his haunches, staring down at her exposed flesh.

She pulled against her restraints and winced at the bite of pain to her wrists. In an instant, she had Leo's attention, and T.J. and Brute were at her cuffs, easing the skin around her holdings.

"I'm fine." She looked at each of them in turn. She'd never been adored before, never been fawned over or taken care of like this. "I'm not going to break."

"Good. Because I'm just getting started." Leo lowered between her thighs, placing his mouth an inch away from her pussy, letting the brush of his breath tickle her skin. "Wrap your legs around my shoulders."

She did as instructed, as fast as she could, hoping he

166

wouldn't hold back from sinking his tongue between her folds. The first stroke down her core sent her back arching off the bed, her hands pulling at the restraints again. Caress after slow, sweeping caress, he tasted her, making her pant and wish she could run her hands through his hair and hold him in place.

"More," she pleaded. "Please." Her embarrassment at the compulsion to beg disappeared. She'd grovel for deeper penetration if she had to. She just wanted more. She tugged at the restraints in annoyance, not caring at the pain it caused her wrists. It provided a much needed relief from the torture Leo was lavishing on her body.

"Release her hands," Leo demanded. "She's going to hurt herself."

She straightened in relief, eager to touch every hard inch of his flesh. T.J. and Brute did as instructed, yet the restriction on her arms remained. T.J. entwined his fingers with hers and pressed down on her left hand while Brute held tight to her right. They climbed on the bed at her sides, watching in silence as Leo went back to devouring her pussy.

She squeezed T.J.'s fingers the closer she came to orgasm. Never would she have thought she'd be relieved to have all three of her bosses around to share the most sensual experience of her life. Without them it would still be profound—her taking a chance and giving herself to Leo—but now her pleasure was heightened, and more importantly, she felt at home around these men.

Each time Leo's fingers entered her, her gaze glanced from one man to the next. All their focus was dedicated to her body, to the way she began to writhe her hips. Their attention was addictive. She ground her pelvis harder, moaned a little louder every time Leo hit that perfect spot, and enjoyed the buzz of exhilaration that came with the flare of a nostril, the narrowing of a gaze or the tensing of a jaw.

Brute moved closer, leaning into her neck. The brush of his light beard was enough to escalate her lust and bring her closer to the edge.

"I knew you'd be like this," he murmured in her ear. "Receptive. Sensitive. And a fucking treasure to behold."

Oh God. She gasped. Dirty talk would send her over the edge and she didn't want to fly just yet. Leo's touch was enough, the brush of his fingers moving in and out, the suction of his mouth settling over her clit. She couldn't breathe, couldn't think with the delicious words flittering into her mind, Brute's breath tickling her neck.

"What I wouldn't give to be between those thighs, lapping your cream, nipping your skin." He nuzzled the sensitive skin below her ear with the tip of his nose. "Leo's a lucky son of a bitch."

She whimpered. Leo wasn't the lucky one. With her thighs tense with pleasure, her wrists held down by two drool-worthy men and her sex on the brink of detonation, she was the one getting the better end of the deal.

"I want to watch you come all over his mouth."

Fuck... The world faded, light turned to black, and she screamed as her orgasm hit hard. They held her down, Leo placing pressure on her hips, and T.J. and Brute at her wrists. She bucked, her core clenching out of control while her legs squeezed tight and her eyes clamped shut. Her breasts were on fire, her heart full and rapidly beating.

Leo didn't stop as her pleasure simmered, the heavy bursts of climax receding to a lesser tingling sensation. Her legs fell limp around him, her arms no longer fighting her restraint and then finally he backed away. She lazily opened her eyes, a smile tilting her lips, and found him on his haunches staring down at her. He didn't speak, didn't move, just continued to gaze at her with an emotion she couldn't pinpoint.

The pressure on her wrists vanished, allowing her to sit up on her elbows. "What's wrong?"

He inhaled deep and remained quiet.

"Petrova lost for words." Brute smirked. "It must be love."

Shay glanced at Brute in surprise and then straight back to Leo. His chin was jutted, his shoulders straight as she stared at him in disbelief.

"No." She shook her head. He didn't love her. He had feelings for her, lusted after her, but not love. Not yet.

Leo raised a brow, his glistening lips parting ever so slightly.

*Speak to me.* She needed an answer, wouldn't breathe until she had one. "You don't." *Do you?*

He leaned down, circled her waist and pulled her to his lap. She ignored the hardness pressing against her pubic bone and scrutinized the intensity in his eyes. "Leo?"

"Hmm?" He blinked as if awoken from a daze. "What, gorgeous?"

"You don't love me."

The side of his lips tilted. "Are you asking, or telling?"

"I don't know."

He licked his lips, casually stroked a lock of hair behind her ear and smiled. "Why are you so nervous at the thought of me loving you?"

Because you're Leo Petrova, the man of my dreams and creator of fantasies.

"Shay?"

Her focus turned to the door as it closed with a click. They were alone. T.J. and Brute had wordlessly left them in privacy.

"Shay?" Leo gripped her chin and turned her back to those penetrating blue-green eyes. "Are you scared that I love you?"

She snapped a hand over her mouth, covering a gasp.

She'd never been here before, not only the sex club or a private room alone with three men, but having her feelings reciprocated. It was always a needy guy chasing her or her lusting over someone out of her league. Now she was in the arms of the man she'd given her heart to long ago, and he was returning it with his own.

"Hey." He gently pushed her hand away and ran a delicate thumb over her bottom lip. "The Shay I know wouldn't cry over a guy."

"I'm not crying." She was just trying to hide her hyperventilated breaths.

His smile grew the longer he gazed into her eyes. "I believe you."

For long moments, they sat in comfortable silence, gazing at one another, her heart growing fuller with each passing second. She'd always known Leo Petrova was a special man. Now she knew why. He was hers.

He lowered his hands from her face and gripped her around the waist. The instant the head of his cock nudged her entrance, the warmth of love suffusing her body turned into burning desire.

"Ready for your turn?" Shay gave him a wicked grin.

"I'll always be hard for you, but this isn't about turns." He reached back, picked up the row of condoms from the mattress and sheathed himself. "I'd be happy to bring you pleasure for the rest of my life without getting it in return."

She relaxed into him and hovered her lips a bare inch from his. "I call bullshit."

He chuckled. "Okay. So maybe I'm a little delusional. But that's your fault. You've made me crazy with the need to make you happy."

"I've been crazy for you for too long to remember."

"A stubborn woman like you?" He raised a brow. "You just wanted to get into my pants."

He leaned forward, laying her softly on the bed.

"Your heart, too," she murmured, then bit her lip waiting for his reaction. Even after his declaration, she still didn't feel comfortable sharing her feelings. He seemed too good to be true. Like a mirage about to disappear the closer they became.

He rolled her to her side and moved in behind her, settling the hardness of his body against her back. His hand found her hip and he delicately stroked the sensitive skin as he nuzzled her hair.

"You're there, Shay. You're mine, and no matter how scared you get, we'll work through it together." His shaft glided through the slick arousal of her pussy, nudging into her in tiny, teasing increments.

"I won't let either of us run." He slid home, ramming into her in a harsh, deep thrust.

They moaned in unison, and she craned her neck, allowing Leo to take her mouth in an equally strong kiss. This time, their connection was lazy and romantic. The pleasure building because of devotion and adoration. He treasured her, kissing her shoulder, slowly stroking her clit. They made love like a couple with a future, not two people expecting to be torn apart at any given moment.

"I can't believe this is happening." Her heart fluttered, her limbs were alive with arousal. Relief washed through her at the way the early morning had turned out. She'd jumped from the cliff and come out soaring.

"Believe it, gorgeous." He nuzzled her neck, never stopping the delicious sweep of his hips. "Because I never let go of what's mine."

# CHAPTER NINETEEN

*L*eo reached for Shay's hand as they made their way from the bathroom and strolled into the main room of Vault of Sin. T.J. and Brute were seated at the bar, waiting, watching them approach. They hadn't stuck around to shoot the breeze. They were here for Shay, to make sure she was all right. And Leo was happy they'd had the balls to do so. It took a lot for any of them to show weakness toward a woman, and that was exactly what they were doing— showing Shay they cared.

"We cool?" Brute took a sip from his scotch glass.

Leo glanced at Shay and raised a brow.

"What?" she whispered.

"He's askin' you, gorgeous."

"Oh."

The tops of her cheeks darkened, making his cock stir to life again. Shay wasn't the embarrassed type, and seeing her flustered was like a shot of adrenaline to his dick.

"Yeah." She gave a breathy chuckle. "We're cool."

"You did good, Shay," Brute offered.

"Oh, thanks." She gave a derisive laugh. "I didn't realize my participation was a casting call."

"Don't get that tiny lace G-string of yours in a twist. I was just letting you know I'm happy for you both." Brute moved around the counter and placed his empty glass in the dishwasher. "Well, I'm heading off for the night. I need to catch some Z's. You need a lift, T?"

T.J. kept his gaze on the glass in his hands, the ice clinking against the sides as he tilted it back and forth. "Nope. I'm going to have one more." He reached for the Grey Goose bottle on the bar and poured himself another finger.

"Make sure you get a ride with Leo then. You're already over the limit."

"I'll be fine."

Brute met Leo's gaze, expressing a silent request to keep an eye on T.J.

"I'm happy to hang around and lock up," Leo offered. "If he needs a lift home, I'll drive him."

Brute came back around the bar and stopped beside Shay. "Call me if you need anything."

Leo could see the adoration in his friend's eyes and ignored the pang of jealousy expanding in his chest. "She's got me if she's in need." He tried to curb the slight annoyance in his tone.

"Yeah, but sometimes you're an ass." Brute slung his arm around her neck and kissed her temple.

"Pot. Kettle." Shay chuckled. "But thank you. I appreciate the offer."

Brute shrugged and headed for the door. "I've got reason to be the way I am. Leo no longer does." He gave a lazy salute and disappeared behind the back of the bar. "Catch you all next week."

Heavy footsteps faded into the distance, followed by the opening and closing of the back entrance door. Then it was quiet. Too quiet. Leo wanted to get Shay home, to snuggle, to talk, to fall asleep with her in his arms. Only something was up with T.J., and Leo wouldn't leave him alone like this.

"You okay?" Shay slid across the stool next to his friend and tilted her head to look at his downcast face.

"Yeah, sweetheart, just tired."

It was more than exhaustion weakening T.J.'s tone. Leo had watched him slide along the scale of self-pity for months now. Each day away from his wife hit harder for the guy who wore his heart on his sleeve.

"Are you sure." Shay met Leo's gaze with concern in her eyes. "Did I do something wrong?"

"No." Both Leo and T.J. spoke at once.

"It's family stuff," T.J. added. "The unending crap that goes along with my marriage."

Shay's eyes widened. "You're married? How did I not know that?"

"We've all got our secrets," Leo murmured, trying to take some of the heat. T.J.'s demons revolved around his wife. He loved her with every breath and every heartbeat. But their marriage had changed over the years, leading to their separation. Each day away from the woman of his dreams had taken a heavy toll, and Leo wasn't sure if the two of them would ever regain the relationship they'd once had.

"Really?" she drawled. "And what secrets do you have?"

Leo narrowed his gaze, wanting to slap her ass for being so sassy. "You already know mine, so stop looking at me like that."

She inclined her head as if to say touché and then turned back to T.J. "Is there anything I can do?"

"Nah." T.J. threw back the remainder of his vodka and slammed the glass down on the bar. "Just continue to make this guy happy." He slid from the stool, released a deep breath and plastered on a fake smile. "Wish me luck handing over the divorce papers."

Leo opened his mouth but silence remained. He had nothing—no words of advice or comfort. His friend had been married for six years. Six happy years. And now he was going to end it all. He hadn't even known his friend had been speaking to a divorce lawyer.

"You can't drive home." Shay slid off the stool and rushed around the bar to grab her handbag.

"I'm fine." T.J. copied Brute's farewell, sidling up to Shay, hugging her around the neck and placing a kiss on her temple.

There was no jealousy this time. All Leo felt was a gaping hole in his chest for the guy who had a bigger heart than Leo and Brute combined. A divorce wasn't the answer. Surely it couldn't be the answer. T.J. loved his wife, and from all their previous discussions, his wife loved him back.

"Are you sure about this?" Leo palmed his keys, ready to leave.

"Drop it. I've only had a few drinks. I'm right to drive."

"No." Leo shook his head. "I'm talking about the divorce. Why don't you give counselling a try?"

T.J. laughed. "Yeah, buddy, counselling. That'd be a hoot."

"I'm serious."

"And I'm done." T.J. shrugged. "I can't spend every night thinking about her, knowing I'm holding her back from the rest of her life. My own selfishness has dragged it this far. I couldn't stand the thought of her being with anyone else. But I've gotta let her go. She deserves better."

"Better than you?" Shay asked, her voice fragile. She climbed back onto a stool and then higher still to sit on the bar. "I don't understand."

"You don't need to, sweetheart." T.J. patted her thigh and made to leave. "I'll see you both next week."

"Wait." Leo jerked his head for Shay to follow. "I'll drop you off." T.J. wasn't drunk, but he was high on emotion. And in Leo's mind, that was a dangerous mix after a few drinks.

"Don't do this." T.J. swung to face him and held up a hand for Shay to stop her progression off her perch on the bar. "Tonight is about the two of you. Let me go. I'm safe to drive."

Leo scrutinized the lines of devastation on his friend's face and the concern in Shay's eyes. Talk about a rock and a hard place. Guys didn't do emotional bullshit. If T.J. wanted to be alone, so be it. He wasn't going to hold T.J.'s hand and spoon feed him ice cream. "Are you sure?"

T.J. rolled his eyes. "Fucking positive." He gave a lazy wave to Shay and headed for the back door. "Don't get into too much mischief over the next two days."

Shay met Leo's gaze, her lips slowly lifting at the edges. "We won't," she called over her shoulder and waited for the back door to close. "Is he really okay to drive?"

"He knows his limits. He'll be fine." T.J. was the responsible one, and the roads were deserted at this time of the morning. Leo was more concerned about the additional alcohol T.J. would consume once he stepped foot inside his apartment.

"That's it? You're his best friend and all you've got is I guess?"

Leo shrugged. Nothing he did would change the shit T.J. was going through. The guy was solid, he always bounced back. He just had a heart bigger than most. "Pretty much. And besides, he's not your concern." He stalked toward her and spread her thighs with a rough hand.

"Oh." She cocked her head in defiance. "And what is?"

"Me," he growled, pulling her off the bar. Her legs circled his waist, clinging tight as he strode for the exit. "Me and only me, for the rest of eternity."

"How poetic from a man who has probably never known monogamy."

He grinned at her, knowing she was going to keep him on his toes for a damn long time. "Not poetic, gorgeous." He placed a lingering kiss on her lips before opening his eyes to the passionate pull of her brown irises. "I've just been waiting for the right female to take me off the market. And now that I've found her, no other woman will ever exist."

# EPILOGUE

"*Y*ou're concocting a plan, I can tell."

Shay grinned down at Leo, ignoring his precise assumption. She was seated on the Vault of Sin bar, her favorite perch to see every inch of the now-vacant main room and glimpse inside the open doorways to the more private areas. "I'm pondering."

Brute groaned, striding around the bar to the sink. "Shut her down, Leo. You know the shit she comes up with is usually a pain in the ass."

"What?" She gasped in mock outrage and frowned at him over her shoulder. "My ideas for upstairs have been nothing but fabulous."

"Nothing but trouble," he countered.

She shook her head, turning back to Leo, who was chuckling from his position between her thighs. He sat on the stool in front of her, peering up at her with his piercing ocean stare. "I don't know, I think I'd like to hear what she has to say."

A ball of pins and needles rolled around in her belly. After a few weeks together, she still hadn't overcome the shock of being with such a gorgeous man. He was perfect. Attentive. Attuned to her needs and desires. The only downer was his reluctance to participate downstairs. He'd told her he wanted to wait for her to gain an understanding of what the club was all about.

Fair enough, she supposed. But it didn't lessen the arousal making her want to double over every time she thought about the possibilities. She'd worked every available shift behind the bar of the sex club, building up her appreciation for the lifestyle. The more she watched, the more she enjoyed. And now she was at the point where she didn't think she could appreciate the sexual setting much more without grappling Leo in front of the patrons.

That's why she'd turned her focus toward club improvements. Vault of Sin required a woman's touch. A little femininity to mix things up. There were unlimited possibilities and opportunities. All she had to do was convince three stubborn-headed men to give her a chance.

"I was just thinking about ways we could make the Vault more exciting for guests."

"Shay," Brute warned. "If the men get more excited, the women won't enjoy themselves."

If Mr. Grumpy Ass thought he was funny, he was sadly mistaken. She ignored him, focusing on the sexy hunk of man in front of her. "Why don't you organize theme nights? Or even a costume party?"

Leo winced, and she tried to ignore that, too.

"Maybe because this is a sex club for adults," Brute drawled. "Not a birthday party for five-year-olds."

Shay shot him the bird over her shoulder. "I'm serious." She used her best doe eyes to implore Leo. The ploy worked in the bedroom, surely it could work here. "You could hold a masquerade party. Newbies are more likely to want to attend if they know their first experience can be hidden behind a mask. It would be less daunting."

Leo's brows drew together. "I kinda like the idea."

*Score.*

"You would *kinda like* any of her ideas," Brute muttered. "Because you're a fuckin' pussy."

Leo chuckled off the insult. "Speaking of pussy." He leaned forward, placing his hands on her knees to spread her legs wider. Her short skirt gave him an unrestricted view of her underwear, and he made no effort to hide his visual inspection.

"Leo, I'm serious." She swallowed over her suddenly dry throat. "I think a masquerade theme would work well."

He slid his palms up her thighs, releasing the floodgates of her arousal. She gripped the edge of the bar, not for stability, but to stop herself from jumping him and tearing his clothes off. Brute be damned.

"I know you are." His touch traveled higher, under her skirt to the edge of her panties. "A masquerade theme could work. It would help to maintain anonymity for those who aren't entirely sure they want to take the plunge int—"

"Just a heads up," Brute interrupted from over her shoulder. "I'm sick of watching you two. From now on, I'll be a fully-fledged participant if you get your fuck on in front of me."

Shay bit her lip, waiting for Leo's reaction. She was prepared to take his lead, no matter what path he chose. She trusted him and the decisions he made regarding their sexual relationship. Sharing is caring definitely hadn't become her motto, but Leo already knew she was willing to let him take the lead on their time downstairs.

Leo stared up at her under thick lashes. "Sorry, champ. I've become a little obsessed with keeping this lovely lady to myself."

She grinned, her ego overinflated. This man knew how to make her pulse race in the most delicious sort of way. He hooked a finger around the crotch of her panties, finding her slick arousal, making her burn. She whimpered, straightening her back, ensuring she didn't lose control. He played with her, holding her gaze the entire time he ran his finger up and down her entrance.

"You're naughty," she silently mouthed, struggling to keep her breathing under control. She was always hot for him. Always ready. Always waiting. Her appetite was insatiable, and she didn't anticipate it ever changing. No matter who was in their presence.

Kicking off one of her shoes, she placed her toes gently on the crotch of his pants, traced the outline of the hardness underneath and then lower to brush his balls. He seemed immune. In control. She loved that most about him—even though the length of his erection was hard beneath her, he didn't react. No matter where they were or what they did, he continued to remain level-headed. At least on the outside.

He became stronger the more time they spent together. He knew how to draw out the best orgasms. How to make her scream, or gasp, or giggle. They were a perfect fit—his sexual expertise and her unruly lust.

"Get your fucking hand out of her honey pot," Brute snapped. "Because, I swear, if you make me go home with wood again, I'll fucking kill you."

Leo grinned without remorse and snaked his fingers out of her underwear. "I don't condone violence."

*No.* No, no, no.

Shay groaned with the loss of his touch, not caring that he placed a forgiving kiss on the inside of her knee to soften the blow. Her pussy wanted to kick him in the balls. Brute too. Leo could take whatever stand he wanted on violence, but she sure as hell didn't condone cock blocking.

"We'll finish this later," he whispered against her skin.

Hell, yeah. She was definitely going to return the favor. It would begin with teasing him for unending moments. Drawing out his pleasure until he was hard and hot and willing to yell with the need for relief. Then she'd go make herself a fucking coffee and see how he liked to be denied.

She snapped her legs shut, almost ramming Leo's nose in the process. And still, the bastard chose to laugh. This wasn't funny. The dampness in her panties wasn't something to chuckle about, and getting home was going to be a humorless affair, too. She wasn't sure how the heck she was going to drive when her mind was obsessed with being driven by Leo.

"Well." She pushed off the bar and landed on her bare foot. "I want to plan a masquerade party." She retrieved her shoe from the floor and pointed it at Brute with a glare. "It doesn't have to be on a regular night, it could be a Thursday or even a Sunday."

"Well, I want you to put your pretty pink lips around my cock and blow me. But neither of us are going to get what we want. Are we?" Brute came around the bar, a scowl cemented into his features. The bulge straining the zipper of his jeans announced he wasn't lying about the blow job either. "We can't make plans without T.J."

Shay's heart clenched at the reminder of the third member of the masculine trio. T.J. hadn't returned to work since he dropped the news of his impending divorce. And yet, after everything he was going through, he'd still spared the time to message her and ask how she was recovering emotionally from her time in Vault of Sin.

He seemed encouraged by her feelings toward Leo. But when she'd asked about his wellbeing, he'd ignored her. She'd even tried calling him, but he wouldn't answer.

"I don't think T.J. will mind if we do the research and

figure out the specifics." Leo stood and came to her side, daring to place a hand around her waist.

She stiffened beside him. Her nipples tingled against the delicate material of her bra and her goddamn panties were still soaked. The last thing she needed was more attention without the hope of a climax.

"Better yet, do up a proposal." Brute went to the light switch at the side of the bar and flicked on the houselights. "That way, when T.J. comes back, we can have a management meeting and discuss it without Romeo's dick playing a part in the decision process."

Leo leaned toward her ear, holding her tighter around the waist. "What he doesn't know," he whispered, "is that my dick plays an integral part in every decision that involves you."

"Not tonight it won't." She nudged him in the ribs to reiterate the rejection.

His huff of laughter heated her neck and his protective hold kept her strong, even though her body was weak for him. She could picture his smile in her mind, the one that lifted his cheeks and brightened his eyes. There was no way to deny him. No way to refute the attraction making her heart swell.

She trusted him, respected, and adored him. Her lust knew no bounds. Their time away from Shot of Sin was filled with laughter, and their working hours were even better. Although their relationship went against the grain of normality, they'd found happiness, and nobody could take that away from them.

She loved this man, dirty parts and all. And no hurdle, big, small, lurid or tame would change that...unless he didn't hurry up and give her a damn orgasm.

"Okay." She nodded. "One Masquerade plan coming right up."

# MASQUERADE OF SIN

*Dear Sinner,*

*You are invited to attend our first, and quite possibly the only, Masquerade Party at Vault of Sin.*

*The rules and entrance process are still the same. You will need to submit an application to attend and gain approval before you pass the sacred doors. However, this time, bringing a like-minded friend is encouraged. Any newbies will be vetted under the same process, but this special occasion will allow them the anonymity to hide their wicked fantasies under the veil of a mask for one night only.*

*In the future, we hope to increase the number of nights you can sin in our presence, and inviting more members to our club is an integral part of achieving our aim.*

*So, if you have a wicked friend, invite them along. It will be a night to remember, filled with pleasure you will never forget.*

*Kind regards,*
*Vault of Sin.*

PLEASE CONSIDER LEAVING A REVIEW ON YOUR BOOK RETAILER WEBSITE OR GOODREADS

## ALSO BY EDEN SUMMERS

### RECKLESS BEAT SERIES

Blind Attraction (Reckless Beat #1)

Passionate Addiction (Reckless Beat #2)

Reckless Weekend (Reckless Beat #2.5)

Undesired Lust (Reckless Beat #3)

Sultry Groove (Reckless Beat #4)

Reckless Rendezvous (Reckless Beat #4.5)

Undeniable Temptation (Reckless Beat #5)

### THE VAULT SERIES

A Shot of Sin (The Vault #1)

Union of Sin (The Vault #2)

Brutal Sin (The Vault #3)

Inarticulate

More titles available at:

www.edensummers.com

## ABOUT THE AUTHOR

Eden Summers is a bestselling author of contemporary romance with a side of sizzle and sarcasm.

She lives in Australia with a young family who are well aware she's circling the drain of insanity.
Eden can't resist alpha dominance, dark features and sarcasm in her fictional heroes and loves a strong heroine who knows when to bite her tongue but also serves retribution with a feminine smile on her face.

**If you'd like access to exclusive information and giveaways, visit Eden Summers' website and join her newsletter.**

*For more information:*
www.edensummers.com
eden@edensummers.com

9 781925 512083